Guess who dropp

"Who?" Kelly said

"Chris," Theo said, looking into the baby's eyes. "As a matter of fact he is in the waiting area waiting to see you."

Kelly tried hard not to stiffen, but her body betrayed her.

Theo looked up from the baby and frowned. "I know you might not want visitors now, but he dropped me and he seemed as if he wanted to see you. Just accommodate him a little. I will come back and kick him to the curb after two minutes, okay?"

"O…okay," Kelly stammered. Her heart was racing a mile a minute and Mark was picking up on her tension.

"I'll be back soon." Theo reluctantly dropped a kiss on her head, handed her the baby and headed out.

Kelly looked down at her baby son again, trying to discern if he had any glaring features that were uniquely Chris'. He was extremely light; that could be explained away by genetics. Even Erica was light skinned. His eyes were going to be a problem though. What if they were hazel, like Chris'? She was looking down at her baby and wishing that his eyes would stay green or darken to a nice brown.

"He's beautiful," Chris said above her head. She didn't hear him come in and she jumped guiltily.

PRIVATE SINS

BRENDA BARRETT

JAMAICA TREASURES

PRIVATE SINS
A Jamaica Treasures Book/November 2012

Published by Jamaica Treasures
Kingston, Jamaica

This is a work of fiction. Names, characters, places, and incidents are either the product of the author's imagination or are used fictitiously. Any resemblance to an actual person or persons, living or dead, events, or locales is entirely coincidental.

ISBN - 978-976-95486-3-3
Jamaica Treasures Ltd.
P.O. Box 482
Kingston 19
Jamaica W.I.
www.fiwibooks.com

ALSO BY BRENDA BARRETT

ABOUT THE AUTHOR

Books have always been a big part of life for Jamaican born Brenda Barrett, she reports that she gets withdrawal symptoms if she does not consume at least two books per week. That is all she can manage these days, as her days are filled with writing, a natural progression from her love of reading. Currently, Brenda has several novels on the market, she writes predominantly in the historical fiction, Christian fiction, comedy and romance genres.

Apart from writing fictional books, Brenda writes for her blogs blackhair101.com; where she gives hair care tips and fiwibooks.com, where she shares about her writing life.

You can connect with Brenda online at:
Brenda-Barrett.com
Twitter.com/AuthorWriterBB
Facebook.com/AuthorBrendaBarrett

Prologue

"**I** can't do this anymore," Kelly said, looking at Chris with guilt in her eyes.

He was driving along the scenic coastline of Runaway Bay, heading towards his villa. He flinched and tightened his hand on the steering wheel and in a voice belying his tension, asked gently, "You can't do what? You can't be my interior decorator anymore?"

"Be your mistress, girlfriend, bit-on-the-side. Whatever this is, Chris," Kelly replied, glancing at him pleadingly. "This is wrong; so wrong on many levels." She clasped her hands in her lap and inhaled. "It should not have started."

"You love me," he said, slowing down the vehicle and turning into the villa's entrance. The landscaping was still unfinished and some men were busy constructing a stone wall. Chris tooted them as he navigated up the meandering driveway. The landscaper, who was transplanting a palm tree, waved to him.

He stopped under the overhang at the front entrance; already the landscaper had planted white roses beside the trellis. They were supposed to entwine around the posts and create a scenic point of interest.

He tried to avoid Kelly's startled look as he got out of the car, slamming the door harder than he should.

Kelly scrambled out of the car and walked around to his side quickly.

"No, I don't. I don't think I do. This is just a fling, remember? We agreed, six months ago, when this whole thing started, that it would just be a one off. Chris...Chris! Are you listening to me?"

Chris strolled into the villa and headed straight for his temporary office, which was a suite of rooms behind the receptionist area.

Kelly swiftly walked in after him, her high heels making an echo on the marble tiles. The lobby area was the last place that she had to decorate and furnish, then she would be done with the job. She had done the ten two-bedroom villas that Chris had commissioned her to do, and in the process had lost all sense of morality.

This job had been her moral undoing.

She winced when she thought about how many days she spent in this very space with Chris Donahue in a sensual haze—hiding away from the real world, and lying to herself and her family.

She leaned against the reception desk. It was not yet varnished, but the furniture maker had finished the design to her dictates. It would perfectly complement the forest theme she had envisioned when she had first seen the space.

She glanced in the mirrors that lined the wall in front of the desk and tried to avoid looking at herself. Her reflection seemed slightly accusing and her heartfelt sigh echoed into the hollow room. She cupped her hand under her chin and a rush of guilt—so raw and suffocating—grasped her by the chest that she found that she was breathing shallowly.

She heard the door behind the desk open. The whole wall was covered in wood and the door was a seamless addition. She glanced around to see Chris standing there with a wounded look in his eyes.

"I don't want to end this," he whispered pleadingly.

Kelly sighed. "I know, but it has to."

Chris ran his fingers through his curly hair and leaned against the door. "You could get a divorce…marry me."

Kelly inhaled then exhaled rapidly. "I have two children, Chris! That decision would have far-reaching consequences."

"I can take care of all of you," Chris said earnestly, now standing before her—his hazel eyes glistening with tears.

Kelly looked away from him and shook her head. "I still love my husband. I don't think I ever stopped loving him."

Her words stood between them and he backed away slightly. "He doesn't give you the love and attention that you crave. I have watched you both over the years. He is so involved with his job that you are a mere second in his affections. I am a property developer. We could build hotels and villas together and you decorate them. We complement each other. You love me too, Kelly! I know you do. I can see you are trying to fight it because of some misplaced loyalty to a husband who doesn't care about you. If you went missing, he wouldn't care."

"That's not true," Kelly said, sobbing. "I can't just throw away ten years and two kids because of lust! I can't. I won't!"

"Lust!" Chris snorted. "I have loved you for longer than ten years. The sad part about this is that you knew, but you married him anyway. I wasn't good enough for you then and apparently I am not good enough for you now."

"Chris…don't." Kelly wiped her eyes and gave him a beseeching look. "I am sorry, okay. I am sorry, sorrier than you would ever know. I'm sorry that this whole thing escalated into what it is now. You are handsome and young and rich. You will find somebody and…"

"Shut up!" Chris shouted. "Just shut up! You accepted this job willingly, Kelly. For years you refused whenever I asked you to work on a project with me because you knew how I felt about you. You have always felt the tension between us. You wanted to start this affair. You wanted a reason to leave your relationship. Here I am Kelly! Here's the reason!"

Chris jabbed himself in the chest, a stormy glint in his eyes. "Leave Theo and come to me. I am not marrying anyone else. I am not interested in anyone else."

Kelly turned away from him, her eyes damp. "I am choosing my family, Chris. Please, just take me home. Drat it, I wish I had driven my car. I will try to finish up the lobby in the agreed time, but I am putting an end to this now. Can we please not discuss this affair again?"

"We'll see about that." Chris stormed toward the car. "You can't just use me and then dump me! I love you."

Kelly walked behind him. "You can't tell him, Chris. He's your pastor! You are his first elder! The church would have a field day with this if it ever gets out. Please see reason."

Chris slammed the car door, and Kelly had to hobble fast to get in before he drove off.

Chapter One

Five Months Later…

Kelly stared balefully in the bathroom mirror at her protruding stomach and grimaced. This was the worst pregnancy of her three. She had morning sickness in the days *and* the nights, and her appetite had fled entirely. She looked like a stick insect with a ball stuck to its mid section. Her once lustrous brown hair was falling out in clumps in her comb and her medium brown complexion looked ashy and dry.

Her issues kept stacking up one atop the other until she feared looking in the mirror. Besides that, she was a mass of nerves. A cloud of guilt followed her everywhere she went, and she even imagined that complete strangers were looking at her accusingly. She was a pregnant adulteress.

At the back of her mind she always thought she deserved to be punished for her awful lapse in judgment when she had the affair, but this pregnancy was the harshest punishment she could have conjured.

She was carrying Chris' baby, and Theo, her husband, didn't have a clue. In fact, he was busy preparing for a series of evangelistic meetings that would last six weeks and had assumed that her wan, washed-out demeanor was the result of her pregnancy. He was completely oblivious to her inner turmoil and the deep dark thoughts she has been harboring these past few months.

At first she could not believe it when the pregnancy test stick said POSITIVE. She hadn't slept with her husband in weeks. He would definitely know that the baby was not his. So in a feverish and half-fearful panic she hatched a plan to have him believe the baby was his. She enticed him to go on a weekend trip with her and then four weeks later cheerfully announced to him that she was going to have a baby. The deception had worked flawlessly. Now, her husband thought that she was four months pregnant, when in fact she really was six months along.

From one lie to another, she was surviving on sheer nerves and every move she made was permeated by the fear of being found out. The enormity of her situation had slowly caught up with her in the last few weeks and she found herself wishing that she could just turn back time.

Turn it all the way back to eleven years ago when she had just graduated from Lancaster School of Design in America, earning a Bachelors in Interior Design. She had returned to Jamaica, fresh and ready to setup shop in St. Ann. Her parents had been in the hotel business, and at the time it seemed like a good idea to exercise her design skills on a rundown guesthouse that they had just acquired beside the sea in picturesque Runaway Bay. The timing seemed perfect and she was happy to add to her portfolio, a real place that she had designed.

Things were going well for her professionally. She immersed herself in the social scene in Ocho Rios, hung out with friends when she had the free time, and lounged by the seaside every chance she got. Then her parents found religion.

For most of their lives, her parents had been happy to leave spiritual matters to those who could understand them. They were polite to all who tried to convert them. They smiled and nodded vaguely to whatever arguments they had to dish out and then sent them on their merry way as soon as it was politely convenient. Kelly and her sister, Erica, had grown up almost clueless about biblical matters.

"All you need is love," her mother, Lola, would tell them. "Who needs stuffy rules from an ancient book to guide you in these times?" Her husband, Fred, would nod in agreement.

Her parents had been known to have thrown a few wild parties in their day, but gradually they were converted to Christianity and started attending church occasionally. Then they started shedding their party lifestyle little by little until Kelly barely recognized them.

Her mother now preferred hospital ministry and choir practice to afternoon teas, gossiping, and themed, wild parties with the elite and the idle. Her father now preferred an evening of scripture searching than arguing politics with his friends. For Kelly, it was simply shocking.

At first her older sister, Erica, who had been living with them at the time, had occasionally gone to church with their parents, and then she too became a Christian. Kelly had found herself in the unenviable position of being the one in the family to be converted.

They tried so hard to get her to change her 'evil ways' that looking back now she found it faintly ironic. Her current situation was now worse than it had ever been.

They eventually changed their preachy strategy because it had not worked on her. Instead, they invited a junior elder from their church to lunch on a day that she would be at home. Her parents had decided that a stranger might be better able to convince her of the folly of her ways.

That stranger had been Chris. He had entered her parents' breezy living room, and it had seemed as if all the air was sucked out of the large space. Kelly had literally stopped breathing.

He was tall and muscular, with skin the shade of warm honey, and piercing hazel eyes. His eyes had zeroed in on her and never left.

That entire meeting is still a blur to her. She had been nervous and babbled like an idiot whenever he spoke to her. She really didn't hear a word he said, but could recall thinking—irreverently—that his long eyelashes made him slightly pretty.

Somewhere in the conversation she had nodded her head eagerly. Later she found out that she had agreed to go to church with her parents the next Sabbath. It was a promise that they held her to and she was eager to fulfill, mostly because she wanted to get to know Chris better.

Leading up to that Sabbath she barely concentrated on anything but Chris. She went over every bit of information that she knew about him. He worked with his father at their real estate firm where he was in charge of property development. He was planning to start a hotel or guesthouse chain, and his family was a stalwart in the Three Rivers Church.

The Sabbath could not have come soon enough for her as she eagerly drove to the church.

The church was in a lovely spot. It was situated on a hill

overlooking the blue Caribbean Sea, and was surrounded by lovely poinsettia trees. She had jumped out of her car and, not looking where she was going, ended up banging her head against the chin of a tall man. He had stopped to tell her that she was parking in a reserved space.

"I am sorry, madam," he said in his husky voice, "but this is…" and then *bang* her head connected with his chin.

She had drawn back, rubbing her hand over her forehead. She had been ready to tell him a piece of her mind, church or not. *People needed to look where they were going*, she thought. When she looked up at him he was rubbing his chin and glaring at her too.

He was the opposite of Chris, she thought at first. He was several shades darker than Chris but was just as handsome. He had a deep mocha complexion; his head was clean-shaven, and he sported a neatly trimmed beard and moustache. He was the epitome of tall, dark, and handsome—her heart picked up speed. Even though he was wearing a jacket, she could tell he had a lean, muscled body.

"I am sorry," the man grinned, showing off a set of startlingly white teeth, which glowed against the darkness of his skin.

She nodded. "I am sorry, too."

"My name is Theo Palmer." He smiled at her again. "I am the new intern here."

"Intern?" she had asked. She only knew of law firms having interns.

"Junior pastor," he clarified for her. "This is my first church. I work alongside Pastor Frommer, the senior pastor."

"Oh." Kelly smiled. "Well, I am new here too. My parents and sister are members here. My name is Kelly Thomas."

He held out his hand for her to shake and she reciprocated, her fingers trembling.

"Kelly Thomas-Palmer has a nice ring to it, don't you think?" he remarked, and like an innocent lamb Kelly had nodded, a grin lighting up her face. "I think so too."

*****

Now, eleven years later, Kelly Thomas-Palmer was sitting in her bathroom, miserable. She was tempted to just go outside, knock on the door to Theo's study—where he was preparing a sermon—and blurt out, "I am sorry. I cheated on you with Chris, and this is not your baby."

Her mind would be at rest and the guilty thoughts riding her brain would stop, but she would destroy her family and her parents would have a heart attack after finding out about her infidelity. Her church family wouldn't be able to live it down and her husband, her dear husband, would not take it well.

She was sure of one thing though: this would be too much of a big, life-altering moment for Theo. His trust in her would be shattered, and his trust in Chris—his right hand man at church—would explode into smithereens.

Even though Theo was a mild-mannered man, calm in his outlook and unruffled in times of crisis, how on earth could she expect him to take an announcement like that calmly.

Why did you do this Kelly? The voice in her head, which sounded a little bit too smug to be her conscience, asked. *Was it because you were horny why you had sex with Chris for days on end? And under the pretext of work go to his house and only return home just before your children got home from school? Were you that starved for sex and attention?*

How could you have an affair with Chris? He was so emotionally invested in you that he refused to come to your wedding ten years ago, and up until the last three years did not even speak to you because he felt betrayed that you chose Theo over him. What on earth were you thinking?

What a mess.

What a god-awful mess!

Kelly placed the stopper in the bathtub and poured some of her favorite rosemary scented bubble bath into the hot water. Her back was aching and not for the first time, she found herself wishing that this child would just die.

Her problems would end and she could go back to her life. But, once more, the guilty feeling that such thoughts heralded persisted and she pretended that the thoughts weren't still lurking somewhere at the back of her mind.

She knew they were wrong. This baby would not have been conceived if it weren't for her actions. It was all her fault, her stupid fault.

She sighed tremulously. This baby was evidence that she committed a crime against her marriage. How could she hope to escape this situation guilt-free, with the evidence of Chris' child staring at her every day for the rest of her life?

"God help me," Kelly sobbed quietly as she clutched her belly.

Chapter Two

Theo rubbed the back of his neck as he concentrated on the computer monitor. He was planning a series of sermons on the book of Revelation and he wanted to assimilate it properly so that his congregation could grasp the meanings and the symbols without being confused.

It was not the first time that he was presenting on the book of Revelation, but he wanted to take a different approach this time. He frowned hard at his monitor. Last time he started at the end and then worked his way to the beginning, but his concentration was not on par today. He could sense that Kelly was unhappy.

She walked around giving him these fake smiles that didn't reach her eyes and looked as if somebody stole her design ideas. A few years ago, if someone copied one of her designs that would be enough to make her depressed for weeks, but he doubted that that was the case this time. She hadn't had a major job for weeks. Besides that, along with the depression, he could see a shattered look in her eyes and that worried him.

He knew Kelly very well, almost as well as he knew himself, and he knew that something was not quite right with her. These days she was distant and cagey, almost as if she was hiding something.

When she had suggested that they go away for a weekend he had broken several appointments because he knew that for close to three years he had not really had any quality time away with his wife. The ministry had so eaten up his time and energy that his family had only gotten the dregs of his attention.

He had made a conscious effort to say yes to her idea because he could sense that she was displeased with his lack of attention toward his family. Indeed, she had often mumbled that church business was his mistress and she was second best. The last time they had an argument about it she had screamed that he spent more time helping other people to fix their family while his was broken and he didn't care.

So when she suggested a special weekend away he jumped through hoops to accommodate her. That the special weekend was just what he had needed—a stress reliever—and that it came with the happy surprise of a third child was a blessing to him.

Kelly, on the other hand, had not seen it that way. She looked stressed and depressed ever since; he was seriously worried about that. She had seemed so happy when she was pregnant with Thealyn and with Matthew.

Theo picked up a picture of his two children and smiled. Thea had turned seven last week and Matthew was now five. They were both spitting images of him, no trace of their mother in their features anywhere.

He glanced at the family picture that they took last year in their annual picture taking exercise and smiled at his wife's serene half-smile. She was the most beautiful woman in the world, he thought to himself, not just outside but inside too, where it matters. She had a soothing calmness about her that belied the passion that bubbled on the surface of her emotions. She was passionate about her family, her church ministry, and her job.

The thought that he almost lost her to Chris Donahue eleven years ago always jolts him when he thinks about it. Chris had pursued Kelly with such intensity that he'd thought he couldn't compete. Chris was affluent and had so much to offer. He, on the other hand, had been just an intern pastor and was from a poor family.

Chris would invite her to expensive dinners and bought her over-the-top gifts, which he could not afford even with a year's salary. One day Chris had even arranged for him and Kelly to spend the day in Cuba.

He had bought her flowers and arranged for violin players to serenade her at work. It was excessive and daunting, the lengths to which Chris had gone.

His stiff, almost clumsy courtship of her had really filled him with embarrassment and uncertainty. His idea of a date was to share his sandwich with her at lunchtime, and a slow drive along the sea-drenched coast to Discovery Bay, playing the radio and hoping that she was not bored.

Apparently, she hadn't been because she used to laugh with him a lot, and asked him a million and one questions about the Bible and Christianity. She had still been searching for her place in the world, and when she finally decided to get baptized, and become a full-fledged Christian, he had been extremely happy for her and very hopeful that they could have a relationship that could lead to marriage.

That feeling had ended though. Chris, who at the time

had viewed him as the enemy, had announced to him, in no uncertain terms, that he had bought a piece of land in an exclusive part of Ocho Rios to build Kelly's dream home. "We discussed it," Chris had told Theo, "she wants to live there. I can afford to give Kelly what she wants."

There was a not too subtle warning behind that statement for Theo. That very day, with a low feeling in his stomach, he had vowed to stop pursuing Kelly. He had stopped inviting her to get ice cream on Sunday evenings or walk with him in the scenic parks in St. Ann's Bay. He started going on his nature hikes alone—missing Kelly dearly, because she was fun to be around and had an infectious sense of humor. She would hike with him, without complaint, enjoying the vast outdoors almost as much as he did.

His withdrawal had not gone unnoticed by her and for a while she avoided him at church. Theo had just assumed that she was getting serious with Chris and was uncomfortable with him.

Theo had even started to console himself that maybe they weren't meant to be, but a church trip that year had changed the whole situation for him. The church had organized a hike to Blue Mountain Peak, a trek that all able-bodied church members looked forward to every year. It was his first year at the church, and he had wanted to experience what going to the highest mountain peak in Jamaica would be like. He had looked at the sign-up list and saw that quite a few church members had expressed an interest, from old Sister Gwendolyn, at 80 years old, to young Carter at 8, and then he saw Kelly Thomas.

After seeing Kelly's name, he had frantically scanned the list to see if Chris' name was on it, but it wasn't. Theo had never before looked forward to a trip like he did that one, and indeed it was life changing. He had gotten the chance to really talk with Kelly out in nature with no trappings of wealth, and no competition from Chris for her attention. She had confessed to him that she was disappointed that he had stopped asking her out.

By the third day, when they reached the peak, he had proposed. To him it was a now-or-never situation. She'd said yes eagerly, with stars in her eyes and a look of love so melting that he still felt faint tingles whenever he recalled the experience.

Their engagement had created quite an excitement among the church brethren. They got married six months later. Chris didn't attend, though he was invited.

For several years after that Chris stayed away from the Three Rivers Church. He gave up his posts and went into hiding, but five years later he returned and avoided all references to the past. It was as if it never happened, and Theo always felt uncomfortable bringing it up. After all, he was the one who got the girl. He was gracious in his win.

It still bothered him that Chris had not yet found a wife to settle down with. Chris studiously avoided the topic of marriage and spurned the advances made on him by the church sisters.

Theo had become slightly concerned when Chris and Kelly worked on a project a few months ago. He always had a sneaking suspicion that Chris was still obsessed with Kelly but Kelly had fanned away his concerns, and he had not wanted to seem like a jealous husband. She loved her job and the assignment with Chris had been a very lucrative one for her.

Theo put the family photo back on the desk and smiled. His mind was not functioning as it should today, and the walk down memory lane left him slightly discomfited.

He got up and played the song 'Order My Steps in Your

Word' on his piano. Singing softly, he tried hard to regain focus on his sermon.

Chapter Three

For the next three months, Kelly avoided her family, and rarely went to church. She felt sick most of the time anyway. It was not shaping up to be a happy pregnancy at all, and she was mentally and physically exhausted. Her sister, Erica, was not pleased with her avoidance tactics and had arrived on her doorstep Tuesday afternoon with a knowing gleam in her eye. Kelly had waddled to open the door and looked at her sister warily.

"Why are you suddenly so unavailable?" Erica challenged her.

Before Kelly could answer, Erica breezed into the house and headed for the back patio—her short, stocky body bristling with rage. "If I told a stranger that we go to the same church, share the same parents, and that I baby-sit your children whenever I am free and you want a break, they would not believe me!"

Erica turned around and looked at her sister disbelievingly

and then headed for the kitchen. "You must be crazy if you think you can avoid me, of all the people in the world! Well, you have a next thing coming, missy! Because unfortunately for you," she flung her handbag on the counter and started looking around in the fridge for fixings to make drinks, "I am unshakeable."

She mixed the drinks while glaring at a mutinous Kelly and grunted, "Let's go catch some breeze on the deck." She carried a tray, with glasses piled high with ice, and headed to the back section of the house.

She placed the tray on a small table between two lounge chairs and relaxed on one of them.

"Now this is the life." Erica exhaled and then glanced suspiciously at her sister. "Okay, fess up. That is not a seven-month belly. That is a nine-month belly." She held up her hand as Kelly began her protest.

"I am a nurse, young grasshopper." She looked at Kelly gimlet-eyed. "Not only that, I know that something is wrong with you. I even suspect what it is. And I must say that as your big sister and friend, I am sorely disappointed."

"What's wrong with me?" Kelly spluttered. "What are you talking about?"

"I waited nearly a year for you to tell me your deep dark secret, but I can't take it one day more."

Erica put down the glass she was drinking from. The view from the deck was a 180-degree ocean vista. The bright blue skies and ocean seemed to meld into one. A little breeze swept across the deck, cooling down the place considerably.

Erica stared at Kelly and shook her head. "That denial is weak and sounds guilty."

Kelly grunted, "Leave me alone, Erica."

"Nope." Erica loosened the button of her jeans and wiggled her butt on the lounge chair, making herself comfortable.

"I can't leave you alone now. You have secrets. Where is Theo?"

"Visiting some shut-in members," Kelly said guardedly. "Why?"

"Only because I watched as he drove out," Erica replied smugly, "and wanted to know how long he would be gone."

"It usually takes quite a while," Kelly said, glancing at Erica and drumming her fingers on the side of the chair.

"You know," Erica cleared her throat, "when you got married to a pastor, I admit, I was skeptical at first. You were a bit of a party girl before you joined the church. You were always down at the beach skinny-dipping."

"I would not have called myself a party girl then, I just liked to hang out with friends..." Kelly rubbed her belly as the baby kicked against her ribs. "This child is so active."

"Does Chris know?" Erica asked, looking casually at her sister. "Or have you been avoiding him too."

"Why would Chris have anything to do with my pregnancy?" Kelly asked, her heart beating a fast staccato rhythm against her chest.

"I know you two had a thing," Erica said, sipping her lemonade. "I also know that you are not seven-months pregnant, and added to that, you are acting really weird."

"You know!" Kelly gasped. "But ...how? Were you following me? Checked my doctor's records?"

"Nah," Erica giggled. "I have a fair idea of what a nine-month pregnancy looks like. I used to work in maternity, and though I am a hotel nurse these days, I have not forgotten much. For you to lie about your time made me suspicious, and whenever I call Chris' name you look guilty. Wasn't hard to put the two amazing pieces of information together. Kelly's in a pickle."

"Yes, I am in a pickle." Kelly looked at her sister. "And I

hate this. I hate it. I hate it. I hate it."

"I know," Erica replied, frowning. "I just had to hear first-hand what was going on with you. That's why I had to come over today. You look awful by the way…terrible!"

"Thanks," Kelly mumbled. "It has not been easy. Child-bearing and guilt are heavy burdens to bear."

"Tell Theo and your burden will be easier," Erica suggested, squinting up at the sky.

"Are you mad?" Kelly snapped. "You must be!"

"Have you thought this through, Kels?" Erica sighed. "Suppose this child comes out looking like his father? Genes don't lie you know, and Chris is significantly lighter-skinned than both you and Theo. Chris has those fabulous cat eyes. Can you imagine this child with hazel eyes? That would be a dead give-away."

"I don't know what to do," Kelly sighed. "I think about nothing else for days on end. I even find myself praying, 'please Lord, let this child look generic.' Then I realized that I am just fooling myself. The Lord won't listen to prayers like that when I am willfully and actively deceiving my husband, but I'm still hoping for a miracle. You know, genetics can do strange things. Look at you; you are significantly lighter-skinned than me. Do you think you were adopted and our parents have been hiding it from us for 35 years?"

Erica laughed. "I look like my Daddy. You look like Grandaunt Presty."

"No, I don't," Kelly laughed. "Grandaunt Presty had crossed eyes and big ears. Besides, Aunt Presty would be 60 when she had me, and that alone would have been remarkable."

Then she sobered up. "This child is a boy, by the way. I told Mom this morning when she came to collect the kids for the week. She was harping on and on about what a joy it will be to have two boys."

Erica laughed. "What would she know? She has two girls. One is married to a pastor and screwed up her life big time, and I am just a hopeless spinster seeking solace in triple chocolate ice cream."

Kelly grinned. "You do look fatter since the last time I saw you."

"Yup," Erica said as she loosened her zip and sighed. "I gained fifteen pounds since I started working at the hotel. I might need to borrow some of your pregnancy clothes to get by."

Kelly laughed. "You always manage to make me laugh… sister of mine."

"That's why I don't get why you couldn't share this whole business with me."

"It's too personal, convoluted and dramatic." Kelly sighed and then contemplated telling Erica about the whole sordid mess. After considering for a while, she decided to just unload on her sister. It wouldn't matter anyway because Erica would never tell Theo.

"I agreed to do the interior design for Chris' new villa."

Erica nodded. "The Villa Rose? He was telling me about it after church a couple months ago. Apparently he has several species of rose all over the place. When he was telling me about it I wondered to myself if it had anything to do with the fact that your middle name is Rose."

Kelly closed her eyes and grunted.

"That man is smitten, whipped, totally into you," Erica coughed. "I knew that your working with him was a bad idea. I predicted this train wreck several years ago, but of course you wouldn't listen. You thought you were immune to cheating because you are a Christian, mother of two, and the pastor's wife, didn't you? Why did you do it though?"

"Theo was not paying me much attention. It's always church this and church that, sister so-and-so, or brother this-and-that always needed his attention more than I did. I don't know. I got restless; I needed to feel like the number one person in somebody's life, not just a wife who smiled at somebody's side at church and looked the part of a dedicated Christian when deep inside I was lonely." She inhaled noisily. "It was eating me up, consuming me. My husband ceased putting me first and I became a hanger-on, the sentence after his major paragraph."

"Wow. I had no idea that was how you were feeling," Erica said softly.

"Who was I to tell?" Kelly asked. "A pastor's wife is supposed to be beyond reproach. I am the one others come to for solace, Erica. Besides, I married him knowing he had a ministry that would be time-consuming. He is passionate about helping others and preaching God's word. Over the years I guess I felt that I was being slightly petty in expecting all the attention to be on me. I have mentioned how I felt to him time and time again, but I could see the visible war that he had to fight, trying to balance the needs of his congregation with the needs of his family. Don't forget he is also a counselor. He counsels young people all the time about marriage. Why couldn't he see that his family was in danger?"

"I guess he is just too close to the situation to see," Erica said sympathetically. "Why didn't you guys go for counseling?"

"Are you kidding!" Kelly opened her eyes wide. "The counselor and spiritual guide going for counseling! Unheard of..."

"Well y'all definitely need it," Erica snorted.

"So anyway," Kelly said, frowning, "last year May, or was it June? Chris finished his villa and asked me if I wanted to do the interior. I had just finished the Jones project so I said yes."

"Nah, tell it like it was. Don't give me the sanitized version," snorted Erica.

"Okay…okay, you story lover." Kelly sipped her lemonade and grimaced. "This is too sweet."

"I sweetened it with honey… Stop being evasive and talk," Erica said, fanning off her sister.

"Well, I was at church, sitting in my car waiting for children's choir practice to end so I could take the children home; Theo was staying over at church for one of his infernal meetings. Luckily, I drove my car. I was playing 'Ordinary People' over and over from my John Legend CD. The music was playing really low and I was humming along, completely ignorant that Chris was at my car door. When the song was about to start another loop, he said, 'another thing we have in common. That is my favorite song too.'

He looked so debonair standing there with his tie almost off and his eyes smiling at me. For years he was very cold and standoffish to me. Then I remembered the Chris that had made me the center of his world when we were dating. I grinned back at him, more out of relief to see him smiling at me than anything else.

He leaned into the car and stared straight into my eyes. I swear, Erica, I am not lying. I was hypnotized. He asked me how I was doing. I got all tongue-tied and mumbled something. Next thing I knew we were talking about his business, and he leaned over and asked me if I wanted to decorate his newest villa. I agreed in a cloudy haze. The morning after I signed the contract—my conscience kept saying *you shouldn't have, you shouldn't have*. But I went to work, did my thing—only saw him briefly a couple of times."

"So…" Erica was nodding her head. "When did you guys do the horizontal dance?"

"Oh, for crying out loud," Kelly said, struggling out of her lounge chair. "I am going to waddle to the bathroom. If you are still here when I waddle back you can hear the details of my massive downfall."

Erica got up too. "I am gonna raid your fridge, but hurry up. This is juicy."

"I can't believe you are enjoying this so much." Kelly shot her sister a dirty look. "Why do these sorts of things get you so excited?"

Erica looked at her sternly. "My only source of fun these days is food. Besides, how often does one get to witness a scandal so close to home, and get all the juicy details directly from the horse's mouth?"

"Sick," Kelly said, slowly walking to the bathroom.

*****

"So, when's the real due date?" Erica asked, looking up from making her tofu sandwich toward Kelly, who sat inelegantly in a chair in the breakfast nook.

Even here they had a nice view of the sea and the surrounding hills. Kelly still could not believe that they had gotten this spot for the low price they did five years ago. The owner had practically given them the two and a half acres of prime real estate. They were situated just ten minutes from the main town of Ocho Rios and fifteen minutes from St. Ann's Bay where her husband was stationed as senior pastor of the Three Rivers circuit of churches.

"I need to know," Erica said, breaking into her thoughts. "Need to be around for the occasion."

"Three weeks…first week of August…possibly August 6th,

just in time for Jamaica's birthday."

"By the way," Erica said, biting into her tofu sandwich. "Have you gone vegetarian with the rest of your household? I couldn't find any real meat to make a sandwich anywhere."

"I guess you can call me a convenient vegetarian," Kelly said, "can't be bothered with cooking two dishes."

"Ah," Erica nodded. "Things get complicated when you have two, doesn't it?"

"I am not telling you one thing more," Kelly said, incensed. "Here I am trying to cope with this absolute crisis, and there you are making jokes and smirking about it."

"I am sorry," Erica said coughing, "Tofu makes me do things."

Kelly grinned. "You should choke. I would stay over here and giggle."

Erica wiped her eyes on a napkin and cleared her throat. "So when did you guys do the horizontal? You were going to tell me before you went to the bathroom."

"I am not sure I want to tell you anymore," Kelly said, looking at her suspiciously. "Suppose you go to Mom, and in one of your frequent heart-to-hearts start discussing my business? In case it has escaped your notice, my mother is the choir director at church and she cannot keep a secret if it kills her."

"I have not had a heart-to-heart with Mother since last year July when I broke up with Jay Jay," Erica protested.

"So I guess you are due a heart-to-heart with her now then, and the topic might just be Kelly."

"Nah," Erica said noncommittally, "I wouldn't. You might as well just give me the gory details before I imagine them."

Kelly sighed. "After two months of going to and from the property, he was waiting for me in his office. He wanted to ask me about some fancy lighting that I had ordered…

wanted to know if it was energy-efficient. I said yes. One thing led to another and we ended up on his desk. It was intense."

Erica smacked her lips. "You didn't even make it to a bed."

"I am not telling you anymore, you dirty imaginer."

"So my question is," Erica asked, as she polished off her sandwich, "who is better: him or Theo?"

Kelly glowered at her.

"Okay, okay." Erica held up her hands when she saw Kelly's expression. "Here's a tame question: Do you love him?"

"Love who?"

"Chris Donahue." Erica got up and rummaged through the pantry for something sweet.

"Top-shelf," Kelly said dispiritedly. "I am weaning the kids off too many sweet things."

"Ah, Oreos." Erica grabbed a pack and turned around to her sister triumphantly. "I am going on a diet next week, I swear."

"Yeah, yeah, yeah," Kelly said. "I've heard it all before."

"So do you?" Erica asked again.

"I don't know." Kelly replied absently. "I don't know anything. Right now I just want everything to go back to the way it was."

Chapter Four

Theo was reluctant to leave Kelly the Thursday evening of August 5. She was not looking too well, but he had scheduled a long overdue meeting with his elders. They were complaining that Chris Donahue was not doing his duties as first elder and they wanted to hash it out with him.

Theo had realized that Chris was not attending church as he used to, and he had been meaning to talk to him. But Chris had managed to avoid him for the last few months on one pretext or another until Theo had all but given up. This meeting was long overdue, and he was eager to hear what was happening with his first elder.

For the past four years Chris had been his right-hand man—very reliable when it came to church work and very popular with the young people. They preferred to go to Chris with their issues, than to Theo. Theo did not mind that as much, and had gone out of his way to encourage Chris' involvement with the youth arm of the church.

At the back of his mind he wished Chris would find a wife from the pick of young adoring women that followed him around, but every time he tried to talk to Chris about anything remotely personal he would shut down. He was super-private about his personal life, and knowing their mutual past with Kelly, Theo usually backed off.

"Hon," he said, looking at Kelly again. She was lying on the settee, a grimace on her face. "I can call off the meeting."

"No," Kelly whispered, rubbing her belly. "It's just a little cramp here and there. I will survive."

"Then I am asking Erica to come and stay with you until I get back," Theo said, heading for the phone. "She's a nurse. She's the perfect company for you right now."

"Okay," Kelly whispered, looking at him out of the slit of one eye and rubbing her belly.

"My car is still at the garage, so I am getting a lift with Elder Gregory. Take care of yourself and our baby." He kissed Kelly on her forehead and then on her belly.

"Stop giving your mommy trouble," Theo whispered to her belly.

Kelly smiled. "I love you... Why don't you take my car?"

"No can do," Theo said sternly. "If something happens to you, you might need to drive out of here."

"I love you," Kelly whispered. "You are the most caring, concerned man."

"I love you more." Theo stood up, "I hear Elder Greg at the gate. I'll try to hurry this meeting along, okay?"

Kelly grunted and closed her eyes. Theo left the house reluctantly, his mind not completely on the meeting. Kelly had looked sick, and despite her protests that she was fine, he was not so sure.

*****

Theo entered the pastor's vestry, a cloud hanging over his head. Everyone was gathered around the table drinking what smelled like peppermint tea.

"Sister Vinney made it," Elder Giscombe said, referring to the church secretary. She usually stuck around for choir practice on a Tuesday. He pointed to the teapot. "It is refreshing. Have some."

"Thank you. Later I will," Theo said, nodding at the men and two women. They formed the nucleus of the church leadership, and they were very serious about their jobs. He often felt very grateful to this group of people. They were really the ones who ran the church like a well-oiled machine. At times he had a flare up or two within the ranks, but he had never had a meeting to discuss the fate of the first elder.

Chris was sitting in a corner looking sullen. He was aware that the meeting was about him and he was obviously feeling apprehensive about the whole thing. Since he was voted first elder several years ago he had never had any complaint about his leadership.

Every year they reelected him to head of the board of elders, without fail, even the older elders were content to have him lead. They were all confused about what they thought was his defection and lack of communication with them over the past year and a half.

Theo was also confused about Chris' behavior. They were not particularly close, but Chris was usually on top of things and very spiritual. For the last few months he detected a detachment in Chris that he was very concerned about.

"Okay, gentlemen and ladies," Theo began. "As usual let us begin this meeting with prayer. Elder Gregory, can you pray to start?"

Elder Gregory nodded, his white moustache twitching. He

then prayed a long-winded prayer and they all gratefully said Amen when he finished.

The room was silent. Everyone stared at Theo, waiting eagerly for him to start. They were all trying not to look at Chris, who had his arm folded at the very end of the table, a small smile on his face.

"Ladies and gentlemen, this is unprecedented. In all my years of experience I've never been called to mediate in a matter concerning the eldership of the church. Usually this would be your job, Chris, if this wasn't about you...that is."

Polite laughter followed that statement, and when the last snicker died down silence reigned again.

"So what is really the issue here," Theo asked, looking from one elder to the other.

"Well, let me begin," Elder Lucilda said, clearing her throat. "Elder Chris is tardy in assigning church tasks. The church leaders used to meet to pray on Sundays, now that is a thing of the past."

Theo nodded, looking briefly at Chris, who was staring fixatedly at the table.

"I think the problem here is that Elder Chris is in need of a woman," Elder Gregory said in his blustery voice. "I recommend Sister Phoebe as a prospective mate."

Chris looked up with an expression of pain on his face. He had not said a word since he entered the room. Guilt—his constant companion—had effectively made him quiet.

"There is someone," his voice petered off. Ten pairs of eyes looked at him with avid interest. His eyes skittered away at the joy he saw in Theo's. "I think I should give up the eldership for the rest of year; maybe for a long time."

"So who is it?" Sister Sheila asked, looking at him over her glasses. "Is it Sister Phoebe?"

Chris cleared his throat. "It is complicated." He sat up

straighter, looked at Theo and then looked away. "It is extremely complicated."

Elder Gregory frowned. "Giving up the eldership should not be treated as a light matter. Have you been engaging in sexual immortality? Is that why?"

The silence in the room was deafening.

"Sorry to interrupt, Pastor," Vinney said, poking her head through the door, "but Sister Erica just called."

Theo swung around. "What is it?"

"Apparently you are a proud papa again. Sister Kelly is in the hospital."

Theo got up excitedly. "But that's early," he said, his smile disappearing as soon as it came. "She's just seven months along. Is something wrong?"

"No, sir." Vinney smiled even wider. "Sometimes babies can't wait to enter the world."

"Sorry, elders." Theo grabbed up his jacket. "I have to go."

"I'll take you," Chris piped up quickly, standing as swiftly as Theo, "since you don't have a car."

"Oh, right," Theo said. "I had forgotten about that. Thank you, Chris. This meeting is adjourned until next week. We'll consider Chris' request to step down more closely at that time."

Everyone nodded, slapping Theo on the back as he headed to Chris' car.

Chapter Five

Chris looked grim and not in the mood for conversation. Theo was silently wondering what was eating him these days. Was the problem really sexual immorality as elder Gregory had suggested? Whatever it was, it had made Chris become withdrawn and unapproachable.

The fifteen-minute drive to the hospital would pass in absolute silence if Chris had his way, Theo realized. He pondered for a minute or two if he should bother him. His curiosity won out and he turned to Chris, modulating his voice to a more amicable tone.

"What's eating you?"

"Lots of things," Chris replied, glancing at him. "You have on your counselor's voice so I am going to assume that you are in counselor mode, Pastor Palmer."

Theo frowned. "No…I am more in friend mode. When Brother Gregory asked you about sexual immorality you looked pretty guilty."

Chris sighed. "I am having some issues. I can't talk about them right now."

"Does it have anything to do with a woman?" Theo probed gently. "Usually they are the chief culprits when it comes to tying up a man in knots and creating uncertainty and tension."

Chris glanced at him and nodded. "As a matter of fact, it is a woman. She's beautiful and feisty and I love her deeply…" He paused. "I would do anything for her, you know…"

Theo nodded, pleased for his friend. *At least the unholy fascination with his wife would stop, now that Chris was fixated on someone else*, Theo reasoned.

"So who is she?" Theo asked curiously. As far as he knew, none of the church sisters were ever given the time of day by Chris. In fact, when Elder Gregory had suggested Phoebe as a potential candidate for Chris he had found it funny.

Phoebe was Gregory's niece, a beautiful woman who was exceptionally self-centered. She was known to act very desperate when it came to men, to the point of stalking them. The men of the church had made a pact to stay as far away from her as possible.

"I think we should talk about it at another time," Chris said, tapping his fingers on the steering wheel.

Theo nodded thoughtfully.

Chris drove into the hospital's parking lot and released a pent-up sigh. "I am sure that you are nervous about the baby arriving early."

"Yes, I am." Theo released his seatbelt and got out of the car hurriedly. "I am going to mention this conversation with you again. Don't think that I won't."

Chris grimaced. "I am sure you will, but for now let's think about Kelly."

Theo glanced at him briefly. Chris had said Kelly reverently, almost as though … Theo shook his head. Chris was simply not acting like himself.

Together they headed for the maternity unit. It was Theo's third time there as a father, and he hurried to the front desk with Chris walking closely behind him.

"Kelly Palmer," he said to the nurse.

"Room 540," the nurse informed him, looking at the chart. "You are a bit late, she just gave birth. Couple hours more and you would have had an Independence baby." She glanced at her watch. "You have a bouncing baby boy."

She glanced curiously at Theo, and then at Chris and then said, "Mommy is doing okay. A little tired as can be expected. You can go in only one at a time."

Chris was feeling nervous standing there beside Theo. He didn't want to leave, after all, he suspected that the baby was his. Kelly had been avoiding him like the plague; refusing his calls, opting not to go to church. Her attitude was driving him crazy.

She had effectively cut him out of her life and he wanted to know why. He needed to see this baby that was supposedly premature. He had wanted to quiz Theo about it but held back. He didn't want Theo to suspect anything. He wanted Kelly to make the decision to choose him of her own free will. He didn't want to be the one to tell Theo, and quizzing him would really install doubt in his mind.

"Okay," Theo said excitedly, holding out his hand to Chris and pumping it energetically. "I will go in first, look at my newest son."

He looked at Chris. "I am sure you want to offer your congratulations to Kelly as well?"

Chris nodded and then swallowed. "Definitely. Besides, you need a ride home."

Theo headed down the hallway buoyed by the feeling of

gratitude encasing his heart. He was sure that Kelly and the baby were fine, and that's all that mattered to him. He entered the room and Kelly was sitting up, staring down at the baby whose little rosebud mouth was pursed in the cutest way.

She looked up at Theo when he entered the room and then back at the baby. He advanced to the bedside and kissed her on her forehead and looked down at the newest arrival. The baby was perfectly formed, very light-skinned, much lighter than him and Kelly, and he had green eyes. The shock of that fact had him staring at the baby for so long that he just didn't know what to say.

"He has green eyes," Theo said in awe, looking at the little tyke with its rosebud pink lips.

Kelly nodded with tears in her eyes. "That he does. I am guessing they will change color as he ages."

He took the baby from Kelly and kissed him softly on the forehead. "Hey, little one. I am your daddy. Welcome to the world."

Kelly looked away, her eyes stinging.

"So are we still going to call him Mark?" Theo was looking at her with a gentle expression on his face.

"He looks like a Mark, doesn't he?" Kelly said, leaning back into her pillows.

"Oh, yes." Theo returned the baby to her, and then sat at the edge of the bed. "We have a Matthew and a Mark."

"Don't you dare say we need a Luke and a John," Kelly smiled.

"I was thinking it." Theo kissed her again, this time on her lips. "I wish I could spend the night here with both of you."

Kelly touched his hand tenderly. "They'll be kicking me out tomorrow."

"Where's Erica?" Theo asked curiously. "I didn't see her in the waiting area."

"She is gone to get some of my stuff. When she came by my water broke. She came right on time."

Theo brushed her hair back from her forehead and kissed her again. "I was right to call her then. Guess who dropped me here?"

"Who?" Kelly said, touching the baby's fingers.

"Chris," Theo said, looking into the baby's eyes. "As a matter of fact he is in the waiting area waiting to see you."

Kelly tried hard not to stiffen, but her body betrayed her.

Theo looked up from the baby and frowned. "I know you might not want visitors now, but he dropped me and he seemed as if he wanted to see you. Just accommodate him a little. I will come back and kick him to the curb after two minutes, okay?"

"O...okay," Kelly stammered. Her heart was racing a mile a minute and Mark was picking up on her tension.

"I'll be back soon." Theo reluctantly dropped a kiss on her head, handed her the baby and headed out.

Kelly looked down at her baby son again, trying to discern if he had any glaring features that were uniquely Chris'. He was extremely light; that could be explained away by genetics. Even Erica was light skinned. His eyes were going to be a problem though. What if they were hazel, like Chris'? She was looking down at her baby and wishing that his eyes would stay green or darken to a nice brown.

"He's beautiful," Chris said above her head. She didn't hear him come in and she jumped guiltily.

He sat heavily—like a drunken man—in the chair beside the bed. "Congratulations on a safe delivery."

"Thank you," Kelly whispered. He was a green polo shirt, and the green highlights in his eyes made them look almost as green as her son's. *What an unfortunate coincidence* she thought, panicking. She wrapped her son tighter in the blanket he was in and tried to shield him from Chris.

Chris got up and started pacing. He glanced at her hands busily covering the baby and then ran his hand through his hair. "Can I hold him?" he asked her savagely.

"No," Kelly squeaked. "Why do you want to hold my baby? Why did you carry Theo anyway? Are you crazy?"

"If I am crazy you drove me to it," Chris hissed. The baby started to cry and Kelly rocked him.

"Just let me hold him Kelly," Chris said almost desperately. "A man deserves to meet his child for the first time without histrionics."

"He's not yours!" Kelly said panicking, "Why did you assume he is yours?"

Chris sighed and knelt by the bedside staring at the red-faced baby, whose arms were flailing and his little belly moving rapidly as he gasped for air.

"He looks like mine," he whispered.

"No," Kelly grunted. "It's over, Chris. Please, let's not talk about this again."

Chris stood up and headed for the door. "It will never be over with him in the world, Kelly. We have to resolve this someway, somehow. I am not going to just stand aside and let another man raise my son!"

"Just go," Kelly said tiredly. "This baby is mine and Theo's. Any fantasy that you may have of it being otherwise is just that—a fantasy."

Chris stood at the door with his back to her as he debated in his head if he should pursue the topic any further. Then with a vicious pull he opened the door and then looked behind him. Kelly was cooing to the baby. *She is so beautiful*, Chris thought.

That should be my family, not Theo's.

He closed the door softly and leaned on it. He felt weak

and dejected. Out of the corner of his eye, he saw Theo in the corridor heading toward him. Chris pulled himself from the door blindly and went to the restrooms around the corner that he had seen earlier. He shut himself in one of the stalls and cried. Big, choking sobs. He didn't care who heard. His heart was breaking into pieces.

Chapter Six

"**I** am on a month's vacation," Theo announced to Kelly, who was sitting on the patio, lounging on one of the chairs. Matthew was on one side of her and Thealyn on the other. The two were busy touching their little brother and giggling.

"Look Daddy," Thea said in wonder. "His finger is smaller than my doll's."

Theo crouched by his family and grinned. "That's how your fingers were small when Mommy first took you home. I sat and stared at you for hours, with a little fear in the back of my mind that I had taken on the biggest responsibility in the world. That fear is still there. One would think that after three children it would go away, but it never does." He scooped up the baby off Kelly's belly and kissed him on the forehead.

"Hey, little one. You are a week old today. I love you."

Kelly looked at Theo as he stared at the baby. The love he felt for the newest addition to the family was palpable from where she sat. He was a man who loved his children and who wore his emotions for them on his sleeve. He hadn't yet talked about the fact that Mark's eyes were green, or that they were lighter than his and Kelly's. He just loved his child, and for that, a heavy burden had been lifted from Kelly's heart.

She had watched him closely as he interacted with the baby, and she found not even a thread of doubt about the baby in his actions. He was rocking the baby now and cooing to him. Clearly, her worries and misgivings during her pregnancy were for naught.

If only Chris would stop hounding her about the child then she would be fine; she would be home free in this duplicity of hers.

She didn't intend to keep this secret from her husband for long. She would give it another sixty or so years, and one day when she and Theo were in their nineties—and hopefully he would be half deaf—she would confess all to him. But for now she was content to let the matter rest.

"So how am I going to spend this vacation, Mrs. Palmer?" Theo turned around still cuddling the baby, a brow raised.

"By changing diapers and getting up for midnight feedings," Kelly replied, smiling.

"Mmmm," Theo smiled. "I am also getting some quality time with you, since these two will be back in school in two weeks."

"Do we have to go to school?" Thea asked, frowning. "Why can't we just stay here and get to know the new baby?"

"Yes, Mommy. Can we stay here with you?" Matthew looked at her, his big brown eyes pleading. "We'll be good."

Kelly laughed and kissed him on the forehead. "In two weeks you will be changing your tune when all your friends start going back to school. You'll be begging me to send you. Besides, your brother is too young for you to play with just now—you'd be bored."

Theo watched the scene with a smile. Kelly looked so
beautiful sitting there in her flowing maxi dress—a slight
fullness in her face was the only indication that she had
recently given birth. She had her curly hair piled high on her
head and little tendrils of hair escaped the loose bun. She
looked happy; happier than she had been in months, and he
instantly felt more relaxed.

He had wondered about her mood for the last couple of
months, but having the baby had changed her somehow. He
looked down at the baby and smiled. He was getting bigger
everyday. He almost looked like a full-term baby. His length
and weight were spot-on. It was a miracle to him, this child
of theirs. He was unusual in complexion and features from
the rest of the children, and Theo was amazed once again at
how complex genetics could be.

"Guys, your Aunty Erica is coming in an hour to pick you
up and take you to Dolphin Cove. He handed the baby to
Kelly. I'd better start helping them get ready, and then today
I am all yours."

Kelly laughed. "Promises, promises."

He dropped a kiss on her lips and heralded his jumping
children into the house. "Daddy, can I wear my pink dress
with the sparkly things on it?" Thea asked.

Theo looked back at Kelly and rolled his eyes.

Kelly laughed. "Thea, you are going to play with dolphins.
Jeans shorts and t-shirt are fine. Don't give your daddy any
trouble."

"Okay," Thea mumbled, heading into the house.

*****

Looking like a forlorn figure, Chris was sitting in his

parents' living room aimlessly changing channels on the television.

His mother sat across from him and studied him intently. He was deeply depressed, she suspected, and he didn't want to talk about it. Still, it broke her heart to see her child in so much pain, and after discussing it with her husband they had agreed that they needed to find out what was wrong with him.

He was hiding something from them; she could feel it.

Even though he was now a full-grown 34-year-old man, that didn't make him any less a baby in her eyes, and when her baby hurts, she hurts too. Chris was their only son—the last of their four children—and she had the tendency to want to smother him with affection. Of course, it was something he resented and avoided at all cost, but that never stopped her from trying.

Her husband, Harlan, was sitting in the armchair pretending to be looking at a file. The file was the bait to get Chris into the house and away from the work environment because he had been avoiding them there, too.

"So, Chris," Harlan started, clearing his throat, "there is a little discrepancy with the Villa Rose project."

Chris glanced at his father wearily. He couldn't bear to go to Villa Rose anymore. He had foisted off the project to his deputy after the break-up with Kelly. They had so many memories there. If he closed his eyes he could see her scampering through the lobby like a little girl, with a pencil behind her ear and a cheeky grin across her face, or leaning over a diagram with intense concentration on her face. His heart felt sore, and he just couldn't take on anything else related to the place.

Chris let out a sigh. The memories were going to kill him. With some effort he focused on his father. "Ask Garwin about that, Pa. I told him to tie up the loose ends, not that there were too many. The interior decorator," he paused and then coughed, "finished everything. Garwin inspected the job and declared it to be excellently done."

"I know, I know," Harlan said, nodding his head. "I have always known that Kelly was a fine decorator. I just thought it odd that since you were so involved with the place you decided to give up the project just like that. Garwin is hiring a manager to run the place, and you haven't made an input. You usually insist on being included in making such decisions."

Chris bowed his head listlessly and cupped his cheek. "I need a vacation. I think I am going to migrate...do something else. Maybe spend some time overseas with Grandma."

Tears came to Hyacinth's eyes when she saw her son's listlessness. "What's wrong, honey? Please tell me. Your dad and I are concerned."

Chris looked up a little dazed. "I had an affair with Kelly Palmer."

Hyacinth and Harlan looked at each other. "She's the pastor's wife," Hyacinth whispered, still shocked.

Chris sighed. "I think that baby she had is mine." He leaned back in his chair and twiddled his thumb. "It's killing me... eating me up inside."

He looked at his stunned parents. "I know I shouldn't have had an affair with her. I know it is wrong and unprincipled and against God's law. My only justification is that I have always thought about it; you know, being with Kelly, being married to her. Every time I saw her at church was torture. I coveted her for ten years, you know. She should have been mine. She would have been mine if Theo hadn't shown up. Now she has my baby, and they are living together, all happy with my baby."

Hyacinth was so stunned she didn't know where to look. Her husband's mouth was wide open, and she was sure that he was unaware of it. She was a grandmother again. Her heart leapt at the thought. Then the reality of the mess that her son had found himself in seeped into her brain.

"Ah…" Harlan swallowed, "what a pickle." He put away the file he held in his hand and started pacing back and forth.

Chris looked tired and washed-out, his hazel eyes dim. "If I tell Theo, Kelly will never forgive me," he sighed. "There would be no chance with her either. She refuses to break up with him. I am giving up my post as elder, and I am going to stop going to that church. I am not even sure I am fit to go to any church, the state that I am in now."

"No, no, no!" Hyacinth said hastily. "You were brought up in the church. You should still go. But you are right; you should probably go to another one, possibly outside of the Three Rivers circuit.

"So the husband has no clue?" Harlan asked curiously.

"I don't think so," Chris shrugged. "I sometimes wish he knew, and all this could come out in the open. I never wanted to sneak around anyway. I just wanted Kelly. And now I want my baby."

"He's not legally yours," Harlan said, looking at Chris somberly. "When a married woman gives birth the baby is legally her husband's, until otherwise stated. Are you sure he is yours, Chris?"

"Yes," Chris said, nodding. "He has my eyes, and though she had everyone running around believing he is premature I know he wasn't. I asked her doctor."

Hyacinth sighed. "Her doctor should have never disclosed such information. Tell me who it is so that I don't use him."

"Whose side are you on, Mom?" Chris asked curiously.

"The right side." Hyacinth got up, her slim body was

encased in a summery dress which highlighted her still shapely figure. "Unfortunately, there is no right side in all of this."

Chris sighed and hung his head. She sat beside him and hugged him, "I love you Chris, and always will. I'd love you even if you were a murderer, but I don't condone your behavior."

"I know," Chris mumbled.

"I always knew you were foolishly obsessed with Kelly. Why do you think I invited all of those lovely single ladies to dinner?"

"Didn't work," Chris said, smiling slightly at his mother.

"I know," she replied, patting his knee. "I don't want you to leave the country, but I can't say it is a bad idea, maybe you should go away for a while."

"We have a business to run," Harlan said, his hazel eyes flashing. "For the love of God, man, why couldn't you find somebody else to fool around with? You had to find the pastor's wife! And not only that, get her pregnant! I am not changing church because of this! We have been going there long before the Palmers, and I am not leaving!"

Hyacinth gasped. "Lola Thomas is my choir director. What am I going to do when she talks about her grandchild, what am I going to do?"

"Ignore the talk," Harlan said, glaring at his wife. "And you, Chris, you have to let this go. Let Kelly go! Move on with your life. Obviously, she doesn't want her life upset or she would have left her husband. You are wasting your time and energy pining after her. If you weren't so fixated on this one woman your life wouldn't be such a mess. So what if couple years ago she chose somebody else over you? Get over it and move on."

He rubbed his cheek and looked hard at his son. "Listen,

boy. I don't think you should give up your life here because of this situation. You just built your house over at Bluffs Head. Time has a tendency to take care of these things."

"But I am a father! I want to tell the whole world about it. I want to claim my son." Chris looked at his father pleadingly.

"No," Harlan growled. "You want to make her choose once more between you and Theo. That's what this is about. Your feud with Theo ended eleven years ago. Why oh why did you go and resurrect it? You of all people should have been able to resist Kelly. She is married! Marriage is supposed to be sacred. My God, man!"

Harlan ran his hands over his face. A slash of red enclosed his ears. "You preach about it at church. You are supposed to be an example!"

He shook his head and sat down. He was steaming, and though he saw Chris' hurt expression, he could not stop. "You say your son belongs to another man, and you want to claim him…Are you crazy? If you create a stink about this, you will drag the family name through the mud. You will drag the business name through the mud, and you will make our church a laughing stock!"

He turned to his wife. "That goes for you, too. Stay far away from Kelly."

After his outburst, the living room was silent. Harlan looked in the ceiling, a vein pulsing at the side of his head. Hyacinth was fanning herself with one of the files and Chris had hung his head.

Harlan finally said in the quietness, "Think about it." His voice was hoarse. He looked at Chris. "Pray about it and avoid seeing Kelly altogether. Are you hearing me?"

Chris nodded. "It's tough. I never really got over Kelly in the first place and now…"

"Now you'll just give up your eldership post," Harlan said.

"For the love of God, man, shake this obsession. Do whatever it is you have to do. Take a mini vacation to Canada… visit other churches. When you get back, give other women a chance, but you have to stay far away from Kelly. Are you hearing me, Chris?"

Chris looked at his father his eyes watery, "I…"

Harlan stared fiercely at his son.

"Yes, I hear you," was the defeated reply.

Chapter Seven

Kelly was getting ready for date night. Her husband had taken a serious one hundred-and-eighty-degree turn and was being more attentive. She felt as she did at the beginning of their marriage—loved and cherished. Theo was delegating more of his duties to his junior pastors and spending more time with his family.

Mark was three months old and big. His green eyes had flecks of gold in them and looked more hazel than green, just like Chris', and yet Theo had not commented. He loved his baby son, sometimes getting up in the middle of the night to rock him to sleep so that Kelly could get some rest.

It felt as if they were now doing better since she had the baby than they had ever been in the past five years; Kelly wished with all her heart that she had not had that affair.

She stood in front of her closet trying to determine what to wear. They were going to a classy little restaurant called New Beginnings that was all the rage in Ocho Rios. The restaurant had live music and the food was said to be so sumptuous that you had to make a reservation, up to three days in advance, for evening dining.

She chose a paisley maxi dress with striking green hues and held it up to her figure. She had barely gained weight during her last pregnancy and was almost as slim as before.

She looked at her hair critically. Earlier in the day she had washed it and left it to air-dry. It had now shrunken to her neck in tight corkscrew curls, but otherwise would have reached her shoulders—she sprayed oil sheen on it to make her natural curls pop.

Years ago she had learnt how to tame her hair before it descended into frizz, and she was glad she knew the technique now because it looked healthy and thick. She left it loose and finger combed her curls so that they had some semblance of order around her face.

I look pretty good for a mother of three, she thought to herself. *An adulterous mother of three,* the unbidden thought rose up to the forefront of her mind and she quickly slammed it back where it belonged and pulled the dress over her head.

She hadn't seen or heard from Chris for the past three months and she was ridiculously grateful for that. Her sister had told her that he took an extended vacation to Canada, and Theo had mentioned that he gave up his position as elder because he had issues.

Theo had said gleefully, "He admitted to me that it was a woman who had him in knots. I have to say I am happy for Chris. He has finally moved on."

She had hurriedly changed the topic when Theo brought it up, but sometimes, like tonight, she wondered about him. She knew that she was the reason that Chris was overhauling his life and she felt a twinge of guilt for that but also a very real relief that he was not going to make any trouble for her by claiming Mark—he had seemed pretty fierce and determined the last time she had seen him, at the hospital.

That scene had caused her several sleepless nights, but now it seemed as if she had gotten off scot-free. Kelly whispered a heartfelt prayer. She was finding it extremely hard to pray these days because she was living with a huge secret.

She heard the door open and looked up. "Hi, honey."

"Whoohoo, you look gorgeous," Theo said. He was wearing jeans and a white dress shirt that was opened at the neck. His face was clean-shaven, and she could smell his aftershave.

"You look gorgeous." Kelly walked over to him and kissed him on the lips.

"Don't start that now," Theo said, "or else we will not make it to the restaurant."

"We can't leave yet." Kelly pulled away from him and looked at the clock. "Erica's supposed to baby-sit."

"She's here," Theo grinned. "In the kitchen, mumbling that she had to carry her own food because all we have is fake meat."

Kelly grinned. "Okay, let me just go and say hi and then we can go."

She headed to the kitchen and found Erica rummaging in the pantry.

"Miss Fatty," Kelly laughed, "what are you looking for?"

Erica spun around. "You were in the bathroom when I got here, just looking for some mayonnaise and ketchup—and stop calling me fat, darn you. Didn't you just have a baby? Why do you look so good?"

Kelly hugged her sister. "I eat in moderation, and I do Pilates for an hour a day, except Saturdays and Sundays. That's free advice, take it once and for all and do something about your weight!"

"Next week," Erica mumbled, turning back to the pantry. "For now, I am looking for ketchup. Don't tell me that ketchup is on the blacklist?"

Kelly grinned. "I forgot to get some. We rarely have it anyway. Why use ketchup when I have a vegetable garden with tomatoes, go pick one and put it on your burger. She looked in the plate that Erica was fixing. "Is that dead meat?"

Erica giggled. "We humans frown on people who eat live meat, Miss Suddenly-Turned-Vegetarian. Last week Mom cooked curried goat, and she said you had some."

"Were you having a heart-to-heart with her?" Kelly asked suspiciously, lowering her voice.

"Yup," Erica grinned. "We went to New Beginnings for lunch and we both sat and licked our lips for an hour when we saw the owner. I think his name is Winston or Froggie. I hear them calling him by both names."

"Oh, brother." Kelly rolled her eyes. "When is mom going to act her age, and when are you going to find yourself a husband?"

"Whenever you tell Theo about Mark," Erica retorted, grinning.

"Shhh," Kelly said, slapping her sister on her hand. "I can't stand you. Don't like you. Wish I never told you a thing."

"You two at it again." Theo came to the doorway. "Come, huns, we gotta go. Erica, I looked in on Mark. He's sleeping peacefully. Here's the baby monitor. If anything happens call me immediately."

Erica laughed. "Parent trumps nurse. Okay, sir, I will call you as soon as anything happens. Go out and enjoy yourselves and tell Froggie that Erica says hello. He might give you a discount if you tell him," she said, winking.

Theo laughed. "Froggie is married, Erica. That shining gold band on his finger is a wedding ring."

"You know him?" Erica squealed. "You know the owner of New Beginnings?"

Theo nodded. "I know his mother better though; she is married to a pastor friend of mine."

"Drat it," Erica said disappointedly. "He has this little air of danger about him, you know. Mom and I were saying he'd make a good husband for me. I didn't see him wearing a ring, are you sure?"

"Yes," Theo grinned, "he got married almost a year ago to a Miss Jamaica finalist. Can't remember her first name. She's Stanley Winter's daughter."

"There goes my dreams, dashed," Erica grumbled. "I should have carried more meat to soothe my weary soul."

Kelly laughed. "You are too funny. Let's go, husband."

They drove toward New Beginnings, chatting about the children and Erica's perpetual man-hunt. They arrived ten minutes early and sat in the lounge area. There were some instrumental jazz sounds coming through discrete speakers.

"That's my song," Kelly said excitedly to Theo.

Theo grinned and kissed her on the lips.

"Ehem." A pretty girl with a notepad stood near them. "That's George Benson and Al Jarreau's version of the song 'Ordinary People,'" she informed them.

Kelly looked up smiling. "I had no idea who was playing, but I know my jam when I hear it."

The girl smiled. "Your table will be ready soon. What would you like to drink in the meantime? We have so many options: green juice, fruit juice; all the healthy options. The chef's special is a papaya, mango and pineapple blended. No liquor, sorry."

"That's fine, we don't drink," Theo said. "We'll take the chef's special."

"Cool," the waitress said, scribbling something down on

her paper.

"Is Froggie around?" Theo asked. "I got a special hello for him."

The girl grimaced. "No, sir. Froggie is in Kingston for a wedding. His wife's sister, I think."

"Oh," Theo grinned.

"Your juice is coming up." The girl walked away and Theo looked at Kelly. I really wanted you to meet Froggie. He was an inner-city don, you know. His wife is one of those upper crust Winters. I don't know how they even know each other—another time, I guess."

"I really like the atmosphere here," Kelly said, nodding. "So I am guessing we will eventually meet. This could be our date-night spot."

She was relaxing in her chair and drinking her juice and chitchatting with Theo when she suddenly felt a stare. She looked up and there was Chris at the door of the lounge. He was standing beside a statuesque woman, who was clinging to his arm possessively. His jaw clenched when he saw her.

She sat up straighter in her chair and drank him in. He looked so sophisticated with his curly hair slicked back and his burnt orange shirt opened at the throat. They stared at each other for what seemed like forever. His eyes were sending off such deep chaotic emotions that she inhaled involuntarily.

"What's the matter?" Theo asked, noticing her tension. His question was answered when he followed her gaze and saw Chris.

Chris smiled at him slightly and raised his hand. He whispered something to his date and they headed over to Kelly and Theo.

"The Palmers, fancy seeing you here," Chris said a little too brightly.

"Chris," Theo said, pleased to see him. "I rarely see you these days." He got up and shook Chris' hand enthusiastically.

Kelly felt wedged to her chair. Seeing him was a shock, and she realized once more how attractive she found Chris and that she was not as nearly over him as she had thought.

He was watching her helplessly too; it would have been exceptionally awkward if his date had not piped in. "I'm Estella, nice to meet you."

Theo frowned at both Kelly and Chris and said, "This is my wife, Kelly."

Kelly reluctantly stood up and said, "Hello, Chris. Hello, Estella. Nice to meet you." Kelly forced a smile in Estella's direction and then sat down again.

"Your tables are ready," said the pretty waitress who had taken their drinks order earlier. "I requested that the live band play 'Ordinary People,' just for you," she said to Kelly.

Kelly smiled, though she was feeling a little light-headed. "Thank you."

"That's my song too," Chris said, smiling at the waitress.

As Theo led his wife into the restaurant, she felt the rhythm of her heart returning to normal.

"What on earth was that about?" Theo asked her curiously when they sat down. "Is there something you are not telling me about you and Chris?"

Kelly felt her pulse fluttering again. "No, no, nothing. Isn't the décor in here a nice combination of sophistication and casualness?"

Theo watched her for a minute and then nodded slowly. "I guess you would know since you are the one with the artistic-eye."

He watched her keenly throughout the evening; his senses attuned to her every move. She was acting differently since Chris came into the restaurant, and he could not fathom why.

Kelly, meanwhile, tried to pretend that she was not casting furtive glances toward the table where Chris and his date were seated, but Theo could see her and because he was directly in line with Chris' table he could also see that Chris was finding it hard not to look over at their table. *What the hell was going on?*

He puzzled over the matter all the way through dinner and through the silent car ride home. They were both introspective, with Theo vowing to talk to his wife about the strangeness of her behavior and Kelly wondering who Chris' date was, and if he had really moved on. Her heart wavered between intense jealousy, a sense of loss, and a low humming guilt that refused to subside.

Chapter Eight

Theo was sitting on the back patio cradling a drink. The baby was in a bassinet beside him and Kelly was gardening. Thea and Matthew were assigned a spot for themselves and Kelly was instructing them on how to plant their vegetables. It was a lazy Sunday afternoon, and the day was cool with a little chill in the air—it was three weeks till Christmas.

Theo's mother usually comes to Jamaica from New York for the holidays but his year she was super excited because she was yet to meet her newest grandchild. She would be arriving in the upcoming week and Theo felt a surge of excitement. He was always excited to see his Mommy. His Dad had abandoned the family when he was just twelve and his mother had really struggled to make ends meet in the early days.

As soon as he had turned eighteen she migrated to America, where she worked as a practical nurse for years. Her retirement was ten years away and she was planning to come back to Jamaica to retire.

She loved Kelly and her grandchildren and usually took her three-week vacation in December so that she could spend every moment with her family.

Theo smiled to himself quietly, and looked into the bassinet as Mark cooed. The baby was awake and smiling too. He grinned and took him out. He was getting bigger and heavier by the day and at four months he was already demonstrating a sharp intelligence that only a doting father would notice. He cuddled the baby and kissed him—he smelled so good and sweet.

He loved a baby's scent; it was so clean and innocent. Mark looked up at him and flailed his arms; his hazel eyes wide. His eyes were a unique combination of green and brown, an unusual color. Theo looked into his baby's innocent eyes and laughed. "What are you thinking about little one?"

The baby blew some bubbles as if he wanted to talk to him.

Theo looked over at Kelly and grinned. She was trying to convince Matthew to dig a deeper hole for his tomato seedlings, but a worm distracted Matthew. He was insisting on taking up the worm to examine it closely. He pushed his podgy hands, with the worm that was wiggling, in his mother's face—Kelly was looking decidedly squeamish.

All was well in his world, Theo thought. He was so grateful to God for the blessing of family. Many people did not have this kind of togetherness and he had to count it a blessing that he did.

"That boy is going to be the end of me." Kelly stomped up to the deck and sat beside Theo. "He pushed the worm at me and told me to stroke it."

Theo laughed and she looked over at the baby, "hi handsome, I would touch you but my hands are dirty."

"Do you want us to go for ice cream later?" Theo asked.

Kelly looked at him and smiled. "Sure! I like this, more family outings and you spending time at home."

Theo shrugged. "When you were pregnant with Mark you were so distressed and depressed; I knew at the heart of that was my hectic work schedule and me not being able to spend more time with you, so I decided that I am going to make more time for my family. I never intended for you to raise the children alone."

Kelly smiled but it didn't quite reach her eyes. She hadn't been distressed because Theo was hardly home but because of her duplicity—obviously he had been watching her and taking note of her mood.

She sometimes forgot how observant Theo could be. A month ago when they had gone to the restaurant together, and she had paid too much attention to Chris, it's as if Theo had beefed up his efforts to be the perfect husband. Instead of pleasing her, it had the opposite effect—it was making her angry.

Where was this perfect husband when she had been lonely and seeking attention? If he had been around she never would have had that affair. Her little episode with Chris would never have gotten out of hand.

She looked over at the baby and wondered when Theo's powers of observation would kick in and he would realize that the baby didn't resemble either of them?

Theo hadn't yet said a thing, but she was silently waiting. Several persons had commented on his lack of resemblance to her or the pastor and she could see some of the older church members speculating. Of course, they would not dare come out and suggest that her baby belonged to anyone else, but she could see questions in their eyes.

She hardly wanted to take her baby to church anymore and she was sure that it would only get worse. She was living on borrowed time and as long as her husband would have her, she was going to hang in there until it dawned on him that something was wrong.

She sighed and then looked at him again, he was watching her closely.

"Where do you go when you zone out like that with a thoughtful wince on your face?"

Kelly forced a laugh, "here and there."

Theo frowned. "I want us to communicate, Kelly." He rocked the baby, who was chewing on his knuckles. "There was a time when I did not have to guess about what you were thinking."

"There was a time when I was the most important person in your life," Kelly retorted and then instantly regretted it. She closed her eyes. "Sorry."

Theo grimaced, and then caressed her chin with his finger. "You are always the most important person to me, never ever doubt that. I love you now and I'll love you always. I have reformed somewhat, haven't I? I am home by four most days and I have shifted my workload a bit. I am helping out around the house and I am chief babysitter to our youngest. I aim to do more."

Kelly looked at him with tears in her eyes, thinking of how stupid she had been. "I really am sorry, Theo."

"I know." He reached over and kissed her. "You are forgiven. Let's tell our two gardeners that we are going to get them cleaned up and give them a treat."

Chapter Nine

Chris was invited to Sunday brunch at his parents' house, and as he drove up to the house he saw several cars in the driveway—his sisters must have arrived. He sighed. The house would be a hustle and bustle of nosy nagging women, noisy kids, and good-smelling food.

All three of his sisters had come down from Canada for the holidays. They always arrived together in the first week of December, but one by one they would leave by the end of January.

Camille, the youngest of the three, was usually the last to leave, preferring to spend an extra four weeks in Jamaica. She would move in with Chris when her husband and everybody else had returned to Canada. She enjoyed spending the extra time with him so that she could boss him around in his own house.

He grinned as he headed up the steps into the house. Just as he anticipated, the scent of jerk chicken hit him at the front door.

He licked his lips and yelled, "Where's everybody!"

"Uncle Chris, Uncle Chris." Three little bodies hurled themselves at his feet. His eldest nephew hugged him around the waist and he took up his youngest niece.

"At least there are people here that are happy to see me," Chris kissed his niece's face. "How are you pumpkin?"

"Fine Uncle Chris," she giggled her hazel eyes beaming, "Mommy was just telling Grandma that you were acting weird and heart broken when you came to Canada three months ago and grandma said you would have to tell them the story yourself. Can I hear the story Uncle Chris, can I?"

"Yes, Uncle Chris, can we hear the story?" the other two pleaded, looking at him in anticipation.

"Give me a minute." He put down his pleading niece. "I am going to have some words with your grandma."

"Okay," they agreed.

He went into the television room and greeted his brothers-in-law, who were eating snacks and watching television.

"Yow Chris," Keith greeted him. He was married to his sister Marie and was always trying hard to talk with a Jamaican accent; the rest of the family found his attempts hilarious.

"Yow," Chris greeted them and then headed for the kitchen. "Mom, Marie, Fiona, Camille," he nodded to them all, a frosty expression on his face. "There is no story. Do not hatch plans to assault me with questions, or badger me about anything. I had a relationship…it's over! I am even seeing someone new…end of story."

"Okay," Marie said, nodding.

"You can't talk anything around children." Fiona hissed her teeth. "So who was the relationship with, and who are you seeing now?"

Chris sighed, sat down in the breakfast nook and looked across at them. "Don't you think it's less than manly for me to be hanging around in the kitchen gossiping with women, when Dad and the rest of the guys are in the TV room watching football?"

"Nah," Camille said, sitting on a bar stool. "After seriously cross examining Daddy he said you broke the seventh and the tenth commandment, all in one go, and that you have dragged him and Mommy into sharing your guilt by breaking the ninth."

"Lord, help me." Fiona headed to the bookcase in the corner and reached for a Bible. "It is an indictment on me that I have to go to look up which commandment is which."

"Not you alone," Marie laughed.

"Give the boy a break," Hyacinth opened the oven to turn the baked chicken. "He is aware of his guilt."

"But he is an elder in the church," Camille said shocked, "so many commandments broken at once. Have you confessed your sins to Jesus?" Camille asked Chris wide-eyed.

Chris ignored her. "That's none of your business, and I am no longer an elder."

"You are supposed to be setting an example for others. You did lead the church. Sin cannot be taken casually," Camille said, "and before you call me self-righteous, I am aware that I am also a sinner."

"Hold on," Fiona said, thumping through the Bible. "Before you give Chris a lecture, let me see what commandments he is supposed to have broken. Okay." She reached Exodus 20. "The first commandment is 'you shall have no other gods before me…' that makes, one, two, three." She ran her fingers down the commandments. "Seven being, 'you shall not commit adultery.'" Her eyes widened and she looked up at her brother,

"What! You committed adultery!"

"He's not married," Fiona laughed, taking the Bible from Marie, who was contemplating her brother in shock.

"This is ridiculous," Fiona snickered. "So what's the tenth commandment?" She looked in the Bible. "You shall not covet your neighbor's house, wife, servants, animals, or anything that belongs to your neighbor."

Marie still looking at her brother in incredulity whispered, "House, wife, servant, animal."

"Wife!" both Fiona and Marie said together.

"Oh, Chris," Camille shook her head. "You had an affair with her, didn't you?"

"You mean Kelly?" Fiona's jaws dropped.

"He's been living in sin for eleven years," Marie whispered. They all looked at Chris bug-eyed. "Coveting his neighbor's wife."

"The pastor's wife." Camille clarified. "So how is it that you caused Mommy and Daddy to sin?" She was looking at Chris and shaking her head in disappointment

Chris looked at them in half amusement. Secrets didn't last long in his family, he was quite aware of that. When he told his parents what he didn't expect was for them to parade his guilt around and for him to feel so wretched. He closed his eyes and leaned his head on the wall.

"The ninth," Fiona said, running her fingers through the commandments again, "is you shall not give false testimony against your neighbor. How does that fit in?"

"False testimony is when you lie," Marie said squinting. "So he caused Mommy and Daddy to lie for him...how?"

They turned to Hyacinth. "Mommy you are silent around there. How did you lie for Chris?"

Hyacinth shrugged. "We haven't exactly lied for him, just omitted to tell the truth to Theo, I can barely look him in the eyes at church and I have been avoiding Kelly."

Camille nodded. "Since you know about the whole affair and you haven't told the pastor you are like accessories to the crime that Chris committed."

"Something like that," Hyacinth said, getting vegetables from the fridge.

"That would make us accessories too, now that we know," Marie said, "first thing next Sabbath I am going to church and I am going to sing to the pastor like a canary."

Chris opened one eye. "You will do no such thing."

"You need to come clean," Camille said heatedly. "Tell the man that you slept with his wife and then confess your sins to God."

"And," Marie said, "when they break up maybe then you can get your chance, marry her and you two can live together then. Isn't that what you always wanted?"

"Not so fast," Fiona held up her hands. "If he marries Kelly after a divorce they would be committing adultery since she is the guilty party. She would not be free to remarry."

"Huh," Marie said glancing at Fiona. "Where did you get that from?"

"The Bible," Fiona said smirking, "somewhere in Matthew 19, I think its verse 9."

Marie sighed. "That's so sad, now my little brother is going to be single for the rest of his life. You know, I like Kelly and from the looks of things, he's never going to find anyone else while Kelly is still alive."

"He did say he found someone else," Camille reminded Marie, looking over at her brother. "Who is she? And why didn't you bring her to brunch so we could check her out … I mean welcome her to the fold of this loving family."

Hyacinth snorted. "I don't like her, she's too high strung and snobbish." She shuddered. "I think he went from one extreme to the other in choosing this girl. She is the complete opposite of Kelly. I think she's obnoxious, though I've met her only once."

"What's her name?" Marie was looking over at her brother, who was pretending to be meek and quiet as he usually did when he found himself in the midst of their discussions.

"Estella," Chris said smiling; he opened his eyes. "Estella Williams, she goes to the Great Pond church, sings on the choir. She has a lovely personality, don't listen to Mommy."

"Are you still in love with Kelly?" Fiona asked earnestly.

They all looked at Chris and waited. He looked from one to the other, his heart giving him a little squeeze each time her name was called. Was he still in love with Kelly? Of course, but he wouldn't be telling them anything.

"When is dinner going to be ready?" He asked, half smiling.

"I knew he wasn't taking this seriously," Camille murmured. "Go join the men. We have plenty of things to talk about behind your back."

Chris grunted, "Can I get a drink first?"

"Sure," Fiona handed him a drink.

"I am sending in the kids," Chris said to them, "that way I am sure to get a blow-by-blow account of this chat. Carry on."

Chapter Ten

The Three Rivers Church was usually packed on Sabbaths, but it was an especially tight fit in December. Returning residents, vacationers and family members of regular church members would attend the various programs that heralded the ending of the year. It was Theo's busiest time and Kelly stood in the vestry watching as he greeted a few of his elders.

These days she rarely spent time in the main church. She would sit with the baby in the mother's room and watch the proceedings from the television screen that was setup in the sound proof room.

Today she was going to sit with her mother-in-law, Valda, in the main church, but as usual, she would slip away when the baby began to cry. She was not too comfortable with sitting in the main sanctuary because she did not want anyone to sit and stare at the baby and come up with any new theories about his paternity.

Valda had arrived in Jamaica on Thursday and several times had commented on how unusual the baby's complexion was in comparison to the rest of the family. Kelly had been very grateful that Chris no longer came to church or her very astute mother-in-law would have noticed the resemblance and said something to Theo.

"Sister Kelly." Pauline the director of the children's choir came to shake her hand. "I have not seen you around the children's division in a while, but I understand."

Kelly smiled. "I can't say that I miss you guys, Sister P. With two children and a baby with a healthy pair of lungs, I am glad for the break."

Pauline laughed and turned to the older woman standing beside Kelly, "Sister Palmer, I swear you get younger every time I see you."

Valda laughed. "Hello, Pauline. It is a pleasure to be back home in Jamaica, and to see you."

"Your grandchildren will be singing solo parts in the choir today." Pauline smiled. "That should be an extra special treat for you and the family, have a great day."

Valda nodded and then turned to Kelly. "Give me the baby, I'll go inside now while you greet your friends."

Kelly handed her the baby and then turned around—her eyes collided with Hyacinth Donahue's.

She came over to Kelly with a determined look in her eyes, "Pleasant morning, Sister Kelly." She had on a broad hot-pink hat that matched her suit and shoes. She looked so dainty and elegant that for a moment Kelly felt gauche.

"Good morning," Kelly smiled at her.

Hyacinth lowered her voice and asked, "Can I have a word with you outside?"

They walked outside and stood under a tree that was surrounded by beautiful caladium flowers. The breeze lifted

Kelly's curls and she swiped her hair away from her face.

"Yes Sister Hyacinth." She looked at Chris' mother intently, a trickle of fear in the pit of her stomach alerting her to the fact that this might not be good news. Hyacinth had gone out of her way to avoid her since she had returned to church. She had thought it strange and had even wondered if Chris had told his parents but had quickly dismissed it from her mind.

"My husband warned me against talking to you about this," Hyacinth looked at Kelly pleadingly, "but I feel so cut up when I see that woman, Sister Valda, with my grandson, and I am not able to go near him or to even look at him properly. I just would like the opportunity to know him too. That's all I am asking. Is it too much to ask?"

Kelly froze. Her knees felt weak and she felt a faint sensation in her head, she quickly leaned on the tree, crushing a caladium or two in her hurry to find support.

"Chris told you?" She whispered hoarsely.

"Yes," Hyacinth said earnestly. "We don't want to make trouble for you or get involved in the whole situation, but in here," she pressed her chest, "I hurt. I want to meet him properly…I am very family-oriented you know."

Kelly cleared her throat, "Hyacinth, Mark is not your family. He's a Palmer. He's mine, and Theo's. Chris and I were never supposed to happen."

"But it did," Hyacinth said, a steely glint in her eye, "and I want to meet my grandchild. That's not too much to ask, is it? It's Christmas season, my other three grandchildren are here but I just want to hold him."

"Your daughters are here?" Kelly asked, her mind clicking in overdrive, one of the daughters, Marie, had two sons and the other, Fiona, had a daughter. The three children could be siblings, considering how much they look alike—same hazel eyes, pink lips, and light skin, just like her son. She shuddered. "Are they at church today?"

"Oh yes," Hyacinth said smiling, "I got Sister Pauline to involve my grandchildren in the children's choir."

That would mean that Valda would see them singing. Please God, let her not try to put two and two together. Kelly inhaled sharply. Was this to be her last day of escape before Theo found out about her infidelity?

She glanced at Hyacinth and sighed, "I can't. I am sorry."

Hyacinth shrugged, "I might have to tell Pastor Palmer then."

Kelly laughed, a hint of hysteria coating her voice. "Blackmail," she threw up her hands. "First thing in the morning, at church! Do whatever, I don't care."

She stomped off toward the entrance of the church, leaving Hyacinth behind.

*****

She entered the foyer, which had interior stonework of a warm brown color, and attractive poinsettias in matching gold pots scattered throughout the space. Usually the décor would have a calming effect on her but even after inhaling and exhaling rapidly, the feeling of panic persisted. She tried to calm her nerves, but she felt jumpy and anxious. For the past two days she was walking on a knife's edge, first with her mother-in-law and now Hyacinth.

Hyacinth was the least likely blackmailer she thought, but now here she was at church threatening to tell her husband the truth.

If he wasn't going to preach today, she would run around to the vestry and confess to him first, but then again, the fallout that she envisioned it would cause always held her back. Today might just be her Waterloo.

"Looking great in red, Sister Kelly." Erica came behind her.

Kelly jumped, "Oh, it's you."

"Yes me," Erica felt her cheek. "Are you feverish or something? You look spooked."

"Can you believe that Hyacinth Donahue just threatened to tell Theo that Mark is not his child?"

Erica gasped, "She knows?"

"Yes," Kelly said in frustration. "It seems as if Chris went and blabbed to his parents."

Erica whistled, "That woman is going to hound you. The whole clan will want to have something to do with your child."

"That's not all," Kelly whispered fiercely, "her grandchildren, all three of them, will be singing on the choir today and you know how much they look alike."

"Mmmm," Erica murmured, "why is that a big deal, nobody in their right mind would conclude that your baby is a Donahue just by that."

"Yes they will," Kelly's hands and lips started to tremble, "Valda is here, she has been mumbling all week about the baby's lack of resemblance to anybody in her family. I am doomed," Kelly whimpered.

"You are paranoid," Erica whispered back, waving to a couple that had just entered the foyer. "Pull yourself together."

"I can't," Kelly shook her head. "I am getting it from all sides. My husband is going to leave me and take away my children. The whole world is going to know that I had an affair. The Donahues will take away my baby and you and Mom will send me to the mental hospital."

Erica chuckled at the last statement.

"Stop laughing," Kelly said, forcing a smile at a church

sister who was looking in their direction. "God is punishing me for all of this, you wait and see…I'll be punished so badly. I think I am losing my mind. Why is it that today, of all days, Hyacinth Donahue had to accost me in the parking lot."

"She's jealous," Erica said glancing around. "Theo's mother is getting grandmotherly privileges and she isn't."

"I never thought of that," Kelly had tears in her eyes. "I am going home."

"No you are not," Erica grabbed her arm. "We are going to the ladies room. You are going to wipe those tears, and then walk confidently into church, we are going to sit beside Valda and thwart every suggestion that she makes about anything concerning your child's paternity."

Ten minutes later they entered church. It took Kelly all of five minutes to get composed and another five for Erica to convince her to stay. Kelly almost ran outside when she saw that Valda was sitting in the same pew with Chris' sisters and their spouses.

"Uh oh," Erica had whispered. "Chin up, don't worry."

Kelly smiled politely at everyone and sat beside Valda but the row was so full that Erica had to sit behind them. Her one ally was out of earshot and that contributed to Kelly's unease even more.

Chris' sister, Marie, kept glancing over at the baby and his other sister, Fiona, was looking at her fixatedly, as if she had seen a ghost. Kelly could barely go through the motions of worship, she felt as if she was in a war and surrounded by hostile enemy.

The platform party entered the podium and she could barely meet Theo's eyes. He was staring at her with a slight frown and she wondered feverishly if Hyacinth had gotten to him first.

She felt sick to her stomach and almost forgot to open her Bible for the scripture reading at the prompting of the person at the podium; a timely poke from Erica had snapped her out of it but she had taken up her hymnal instead.

All of this had not gone unnoticed by her husband who was watching her keenly. They sat down for the special song, which was done by the children's choir. She couldn't even drum up a smile for Thealyn and Matthew who were in the front row—her eyes kept darting to the Donahue children in the front.

Valda whispered to her, "They look adorable in their purple and white choir robes."

Kelly nodded and forced a smile. At least Valda hadn't noticed anything unique about the Donahue children.

She breathed a sigh of relief but quickly came on edge again when Mark began to cry.

"I'll take him to the mother's room," Valda said, and got up before Kelly could say that she would do it.

Kelly watched as Camille, Chris' favorite and closest sister, got up to follow her. *Where is she going?* Kelly thought in a panic, she hoped it was not to examine her baby more closely.

The agony of it all hit her and she didn't realize that she missed the whole children's song until the church said "Amen," snapping her out of her feverish imaginings and self-agonizing.

Chapter Eleven

The sermon was a very well researched one based on covetousness. Usually when her husband preached Kelly would be very alert and listened carefully to what he said. Theo outlined the meaning of covetousness, which is an extreme desire to acquire or possess, wanting what others had and not being content with your own.

He used a projector for his sermons to emphasize his points. He frequently glanced at Kelly, who had now schooled her features into a parody of contentment. She wished she could see her own expression to see if she was properly imitating contentment, because she was as far from content as anyone could be.

Her mind was in the mother's room. Neither Camille nor Valda had returned and she was getting anxious as each second ticked by. She couldn't take it any longer and she got up to go see what was keeping her mother-in-law.

She entered the room at the front of the church—to the

right of the foyer—and pushed the door.

Valda was seated in one of the padded chairs and was watching the sermon intently and Camille was holding her baby.

Kelly felt the building spin a little and she slumped onto a nearby chair, dazed. The mother's room was empty but for the three adults.

"Oh, there you are," Valda said, smiling. "I could not get him to calm down," she pointed to the baby, "so Camille here volunteered. It seemed to have worked."

Kelly nodded, trying hard not to look directly at Camille. "You can go back into church now, Valda. I'll stay with him."

"Okay, if you are sure," Valda said. "You don't look so well."

"I am fine," Kelly went over to Camille, "just a bad headache coming on."

"Then maybe you should just let me baby-sit a while then," Camille said gazing at Kelly intently.

"Okay, I'll sit here but you go on in, Valda."

Valda smiled and left the mother's room.

The only sounds that could be heard were the cooing of the baby and the sermon coming from the television.

Kelly avoided Camille's eyes and at first Camille did not say a word.

"How are you getting away with this?" Camille calmly asked after placing the now sleeping baby in the bassinet that Kelly had placed in the mother's room in anticipation of going there for solitude.

Kelly looked at Camille and shrugged. "What on earth are you talking about?"

Camille half-smiled. "Your husband must be blind."

Kelly stiffened. "Please stop, this is none of your business."

"My brother, my business. My nephew, my business!"

"What's the matter with you people." Kelly got up. "First your mother, now you. That baby belongs to me and my husband. I should not have to be defending that."

"No you shouldn't," Camille said quietly, "but you and Chris had that little affair and now here you are defending yourself to me. You know we discussed this last Sunday and he never brought up the fact that he got you pregnant, but Marie, Fiona, and I took one look at the baby and knew we were related to him."

"Leave it alone!" Kelly sat back down and closed her eyes. "I am handling this the best way I know how."

"No, you are not. You have my brother hiding away from this church that he has served for years. You have taken his only child and given it to another man. You are selfish."

Kelly widened her eyes, her lips trembling. "No, you are the one that's selfish, you and your mother and your whole family. I love my husband and my children and being selfish—as you call it—is what works for us right now."

Kelly's voice became suffused with tears. "I don't need you and your family judging me. If I could turn back the clock, I would. I wouldn't have worked with your brother, have had an affair with him, and cheated on my husband. I am so sorry. I wish that I could just absent myself from the whole situation, like Chris, and move on with my life, okay! But I can't and I am tired of being judged and dissected and found wanting."

She stood up, grabbed the handle of the bassinet and stormed out of the mother's room. She sat in her car for minutes as she watched her sleeping baby and looked out at the view from the parking lot. So today was the end of the world for Kelly Palmer. Too many people were privy to her secret and no doubt somebody would tell her husband. The imaginary axe that was swinging for her head was on its way down. She slumped with her head on the steering wheel; feeling wretched and sick.

*****

"I am so sorry about your headache," Valda was looking at her with sympathy.

"I knew something was wrong with you when you walked into church today," Theo kissed her on the forehead. "I will make some chamomile tea. You get some rest, okay honey."

"Fine," Kelly nodded, heading for the stairs. The master bedroom was just to the left but she felt as if she was seeing two doors. She really had gotten a monstrous headache from all that over thinking and stress.

She kicked off her heels and slumped onto the bed the moment she reached the room. She would have driven home from church but her hands had been trembling and they had driven the one car, so she had to wait. Thankfully, Theo had not taken as long to leave church as he always did, coming to find her, after the service, as soon as he could.

When he found her in the car with beads of sweat on her upper lip and her head in her hands he had concluded that she was suffering from one of her infrequent headaches. Unfortunately, her headaches usually occurred when she was undergoing undue stress and Theo knew that.

She looked up when Theo entered the room with her tea. He drew the curtains, leaving the room in semi-darkness and whispered, "hush my love, you will soon be better."

He gave her the tea and gently massaged her feet while she drank it. "You have such perfectly arched feet," he said soothingly.

"Thanks," Kelly murmured, the effect of the tea and the massage calming her nerves, somewhat.

"You looked extremely beautiful today," Theo whispered, "but I knew that something was wrong. You looked uncomfortable, like you were on the verge of crying. I wanted to come down from the platform and give you a hug."

He took the empty cup from Kelly and cuddled her to his chest, "I hate when you are in pain Kelly...wish I could suffer through your headache instead."

He waited for her breathing to become regular before he moved; laying her head gently against the pillow and staring down at her. Her eyelashes were short and thick like a stumpy curtain; he had always found them fascinating, as he did anything that belonged to Kelly.

Her nose was short and straight and her lips were full and red. It was the first thing he had noticed about her. It had taken him several dates to ask her if the shade was real or if it was a particular shade of lipstick. He smiled now as he looked at her intently. She had laughed and said they are real. He didn't believe her, so he had kissed them to settle the question.

He kissed her lips softly now and sighed. He wasn't a fool, something was bothering Kelly. Exactly what it was he was clueless about but he was tired of waiting around to find out. He would tackle what was causing her such mental anguish and get to the bottom of it; maybe he could help her with whatever it was.

He got up and quietly closed the door. The kids were in the living room watching a Bible story on DVD, and his mother was in the kitchen reheating the food.

"How is she doing?" Valda glanced at him.

"Sleeping," Theo grabbed his head and braced his feet apart. "Can I help?"

"No," Valda said. "I have everything under control. The tofu and beans, and barbecued gluten are heating up in the oven...the rice is in the microwave."

"Where's the baby?" Theo asked suddenly concerned.

"Sleeping," Valda said then paused, "Theo I am not one to pry or anything but...I mean...this baby looks nothing like us."

Theo shook his head. "Not that again Mom."

Valda looked at him intently, "This baby resembles that girl I saw today in the mother's room, Camille Donahue. You should have seen the possessive way she was looking at the baby."

Theo sat down on a stool beside the counter. "I agree that he is lighter than both Kelly and me, but families are like that, there are several shades of color in our gene pool, several races and all of that mixed up."

"Who in Kelly's family has hazel eyes with green flecks?" Valda asked curiously. "Just name one person."

Theo scratched his head. "Nobody that I know of, but I don't know all of her family."

His mother made a harrumph sound. "Maybe you should investigate this some more. Maybe the baby was switched at the hospital. I heard of a case the other day where the hospital messed up and gave two families the wrong babies."

"There was no mix up," Theo said frowning. "That's our baby."

"Or maybe it's not." Valda bent down to check on the protein in the oven and missed the look of fear that crossed her son's face.

.

Chapter Twelve

"**A**re you sure that you want to drive all the way to Kingston with the baby?" Theo was asking Kelly as he sipped his tea. He was sitting on the counter stool going through is Monday morning routine of scrolling through all the emails he had received over the weekend.

Kelly was now standing in the same spot that his mother had stood two days ago when she had the nerve to suggest that this last baby was not his. It was riding at the back of his mind, the insidious thoughts hanging on to the fringes of his consciousness day and night, but he managed to brush them away with a Herculean effort.

"I am sure." Kelly took out a loaf of whole wheat bread from the fridge. "Your mother is staying overnight in Montego Bay with Thea and Matthew. You are going to the community leaders convention…you can't carry a baby there, and my mother and sister are going to some soap making seminar or the other. Those two are as thick as thieves."

Theo nodded. "Are you sure you don't want to wait until tomorrow, we can make it a family trip."

"Nope," Kelly grinned. "I start working at the Peterson's tomorrow. They are redecorating their son's room...it's just a three-day job. I am going just to get my supplies in Kingston...I already called it in. When I get back, I'll call my people, get them moving and then I will be done."

"Keep in touch," Theo said hopping off the stool, "but not when you are driving."

Kelly saluted, "Aye aye captain."

Theo kissed her, grabbed his jacket and left the house.

On her way to Kingston, Kelly popped her favorite CD into the car radio and started singing along with the songs; the baby cooed in the car seat as she navigated the twists and turns.

She turned the radio higher when her favorite song *Wake Up Everybody* by *Teddy Pendergrass* started to play.

She sang it so loudly that the baby started to cry; she slowed the car a bit and turned the music down. "Sorry baby," she said looking at him. "I am just letting off steam."

She crawled to a stop at the Flat Bridge stoplight. She gazed down into the blue green depths of the river. The color was a richer version of her multicolored blouse and she grinned. "No matter how men try, they cannot capture the beautiful colors of nature exactly, can they, Mark?"

The baby cooed and clapped his hands.

"There ya go," She looked back at him. "Sorry for scaring you earlier. I certainly hope it wasn't my voice that scared you?"

She laughed when he yawned.

*****

She entered the city of Kingston with its hustle and bustle and traffic jams at a quarter to ten. Her business took her approximately two hours and she packed up the car with her purchases.

"Lunch time for me," she said to the baby, who had already gotten a bottle, "then we are going to head back home. That wasn't so bad, was it?"

She decided to go to Wendy's in New Kingston. Even though Kingston, in December was slightly cooler than normal, she was looking forward to sitting in an air-conditioned restaurant and eating a salad or a baked potato, and a yummy dessert.

When she drove up to the entrance of the restaurant; it took her a while to get the baby out of the car and all the paraphernalia that she would need to go into the restaurant.

"Traveling with a baby takes you twice the time," she said out loud to the baby, who was blowing bubbles at her.

"It should be," Chris said behind her, she almost dropped the baby in fright.

"Chris!" She spun around. "What on earth!"

Chris grinned, "I was heading to the bank across the street when I saw you get out of the vehicle. I couldn't believe it when I saw that you were alone. I nearly ran into traffic."

"I came to get supplies for a project I'm starting tomorrow." She eyed him up and down. "You look good."

"You look better," he said, softly, "Can I have lunch with you two?"

Kelly sighed, "Why not?"

She locked the car and they headed into the restaurant together.

"I'll order for you," Chris said.

"Baked potatoes and garden salad," Kelly told him absently as she placed the baby in the bassinet.

Chris paused, looking down at the baby. "He has gotten so big since the last time I saw him."

Kelly looked up at Chris and then back down at the baby. He eventually moved away and she breathed a sigh of relief. Exactly why she was having lunch with Chris was not clear, she just felt as if they had so many loose ends to tie-up and talking about them would make it easier.

When Chris eventually came back with their orders she was scrolling through her PDA and checking that she had everything on her list.

"So how've you been these days?" He bit into a burger and looked at her closely.

"Fine...edgy," she shrugged. "How've you been?"

"I miss you," he said wiping his lips. "Wish we were together. At nights when I can't turn off my brain I feel a sense of loss so acute, it hurts." He brushed back his curly hair, which had been a little unkempt over the months. "I am trying to deal with it, it's painful."

Kelly nodded. "So who was that girl Theo and I saw you with at New Beginnings?"

"Estella." He half smiled. "Were you jealous?"

Kelly frowned, "no—yes."

He grinned.

The baby started to cry as she picked at her salad, and without asking Chris picked him up.

He had grown considerably heavier and holding his son face to face almost brought tears to his eyes. The baby stopped mid-wail and gazed at Chris curiously.

Chris laughed. "Hey little man."

"Your baby is so cute." A young woman stopped at the table, looking from Chris to the baby. "He looks just like you."

"Thanks," Chris said, cuddling the baby and then looked at

Kelly, his brows raised. When the young lady had moved out of hearing distance, he stared at Kelly hungrily.

"Stop it!" Kelly said fiercely.

"No," Chris said just as fiercely.

Kelly pushed away her plate and covered it. "It's over Chris!"

"I know," Chris said earnestly, "but I just want to know this one thing, if by some quirk of fate, your marriage breaks up, do I have a chance?"

Kelly shuddered. "My marriage is fine, stop wishing for its demise."

He shrugged. "It is fine for now. I just want you to know that if anything happens I am an option. My mother told me that she accosted you in the parking lot at church and my sister told me you cussed her off."

Kelly smirked. "Why can't they just leave me alone?"

Chris gently laid the baby back in the bassinet. "Don't worry, I called them off. I had strong words with them… told them that I was just as guilty as you in this whole mess and that they should give you time. I sometimes feel like marching up to your house and snatching him, you know."

Kelly looked frightened. "You wouldn't do that!"

"I would," Chris nodded, "but I know it would hurt you and your other kids and Theo. These days I am just turning off my emotions; I'm trying to deal with the whole situation. The other night I had a long heartfelt talk with God and I am slowly healing. Seeing you now will set back my recovery a bit. You are like drugs to me. I used to come to church every week to get a hit you know. When you worked for me, I took a hit everyday." He sighed. "I couldn't help feeding my addiction and I enjoyed every last hit."

Kelly grimaced. "I am sorry for screwing up your life."

"I screwed up my own life," Chris said passionately.

"When I first saw you eleven years ago I thought, there she is, my wife. It was as if my heart recognized its mate. I was blindsided when you told me that you were seeing Theo and that you never thought that we were serious. I went all out for you. I was serious then, Kelly, so serious you wouldn't understand. I bought a piece of land on Bluffs Head, started making plans to build our dream home and I got left in the dust for Theo. I almost went crazy."

He glanced over at the baby. "I was so broken that it took me all of seven years to heal. Nobody else came close." He smiled sadly. "It wasn't my ego that got battered when you chose Theo," he held onto her fingers, "it was a genuine loss. So when I got the chance to be with you, whether it was an illicit affair or not, I took it. Forsaking my vows of celibacy, forgetting that I had a responsibility as a church leader, I took the opportunity to be with you. I was actually glad that Theo was so busy, ecstatic that there were cracks in your marriage." He lowered his voice, even though the restaurant was not crowded. "I wanted you completely but I never really had you, did I?"

Feeling them tingle, Kelly dragged her hands away. She was attracted to Chris, there was no denying that, but she loved Theo and suddenly a wave of intense regret swept over her. She had been quite stupid to have had an affair.

The affair was based on a crush. As she had learned, to her detriment, physical attraction was powerful enough to blindside someone for a while but true abiding love, the love that came with knowing somebody over time; living with them; sharing experiences with them, that was more abiding. That was what she had for Theo.

What she felt for Chris was a raw, untamed fire. It was suddenly clear to her that what she felt for Chris would fizzle out if they ever got together. She would wake up guilty and depressed everyday. Eventually, the sex without the substance would pall and they would end up hating each other.

She looked hard at Chris for the first time, without the scales of lust blinding her eyes and realized that she broke her husband's trust; she shattered her commitment to him and her family because of old fashioned lust. She had given into that visceral emotion that had brought empires down and smashed family ties—it never lasts; it never endures.

Suddenly she realized the enormity of what she had done. She had compounded one mistake atop another until here she was, sitting across from her ex-lover and their baby, and was lying to her husband.

She closed her eyes and then opened them, "Chris."

"Mmm," he said looking back at her.

"I had a huge crush on you years ago and it has played a part in my present day troubles. I never did put it to rest you know…that feeling I had when I first saw you. I guess, at the back of mind, I wanted to be with you just to see what it would have been like, but I don't love you, not the way I love Theo. I never did. I know words are not adequate to say just how much I regret that this ever happened."

Chris looked away from her with a pained look in his eyes. He then sighed and shrugged. "As I said, I am trying to move on. Maybe one day I will find another love. Maybe one day you'll tell Mark the truth about his father and we'll forge some form of relationship."

She shook her head. "I am not even thinking about that right now."

*****

The drive back to St. Ann was not as turbulent for Kelly. It was as if something that was broken in her head was finally fixed, and she seriously contemplated driving home and telling all to her husband, but the possible repercussions of her actions made her recoil. Once the bonds of trust were broken in a relationship it would never be the same. She couldn't bear to think of the devastation that would follow in the wake of her confession to Theo.

She had admitted a third party and another family into their relationship. How does one recover from that?

If she were on the receiving end of such news she knew that it would devastate her; drive her crazy.

Wasn't there some rule that said that your spouse didn't need to know everything? That one should just leave well enough alone and that some secrets were better not exposed. After all, what one didn't know wouldn't hurt them.

In theory that was fine but the reality was pure torture. How did some married women live with themselves for years knowing that a child—born as a result of an affair—did not belong to their spouse?

How did they live with it and not give something away?

She could barely breathe from the pressure of the guilt surrounding her. Each day it got worse. Each day the guilt stung a little deeper; her wounds gapped a little wider and she was left floundering in the quagmire of her sins.

"Lord, help me," she whispered.

*****

When she entered the town of Ocho Rios she decided to visit her parents at Hibiscus Close, a scenic spot overlooking the town of Ocho Rios. The light was fading fast and it was barely five o'clock.

She looked at the clock on the dashboard. Theo had called her twice to find out where she was and to let her know that he was stuck in a church council meeting and would be home late.

She turned left into her parent's driveway and parked behind Erica's car. Her mother was a free spirit who planted herbs and medicinal plants, played the harp, and went to soap making and flower arranging classes.

She was fifty-nine years old but looked at least ten years younger. It was often a source of irritation to Erica that strangers assumed that Erica was the mother and Lola was the daughter whenever they went out together.

Her father was the opposite. He was a serious—more of a logical thinker—and though he had a law degree, he never practiced, choosing instead to run a chain of successful supermarkets on the North Coast of the Island. He lives a retirees dream, playing golf all week and rarely checking in on his businesses.

When he did check on the books, his eagle eyes would catch the slightest mistake, so his managers were really conscientious with their accounting. Kelly looked for his car but didn't see it. More than likely, he was off playing golf.

Kelly took the baby from the car and shut the door.

"Bring my grandchild here." Lola was at the front door in a flowing summer dress, her eyes sparkling. Erica was standing behind her and the two were grinning.

"I am going to bathe him in a combination of shea butter, chamomile, and rose oil."

Kelly rolled her eyes. "I hope all those three are good for bathing." She handed over the baby. "I don't want you experimenting on my child and harming his skin."

Lola took the baby and cooed, "I wouldn't experiment with him," she grinned, "I already experimented enough with you and Erica while you were babies, especially Erica because she was the first."

Erica grimaced. "You must have done something to me when I was little because I am addicted to chocolate. It's all your fault."

Lola laughed out loud while rocking the baby.

"Children blame everything on their mothers."

Kelly stepped inside. The house was simply decorated but her mother had a profusion of plants in every available corner. The house was infused with the scent of her latest obsession—jasmine. The pungent smell was uniquely relaxing and Kelly sat down in a sofa gratefully inhaling it deeply.

"I need a pot of one of your jasmine plants, Mom. I would never have to use air freshener."

"Never," Erica agreed. "Today, in our soap class, we bought a vial of jasmine oil for a whole lot of money. I told Mommy that if we could learn to distil it we could make it ourselves."

"True," Lola said. "We should go to one of those classes and learn to do that."

Erica nodded. "Next year perhaps, my vacation is almost up and I am not a woman of leisure like you."

Lola shrugged. "Kelly you work for yourself, can we go together?"

"Nooo," Kelly shook her head vehemently, "I have three children, one of them a baby. When I have free time, I want to just sit on my veranda and read."

Lola grinned, "I might just drag your Dad with me then."

Erica laughed and toppled over on the settee. "Daddy would say, 'how much per hour is this thing? Can't you experiment with the plant yourself.?'"

Lola shrugged. "Chalk and cheese, your father and I, but

our marriage keeps going and going and going."

She paused and then asked Kelly, "How are you and Theo?"

"Fine," Kelly looked at her puzzled, "Why do you ask, you have never asked me that before."

Lola sighed and then sat down with the baby in her lap. "I know when something is wrong with any of my children. I feel it. I may not pry but I feel it."

"Yeah right," Erica snorted, "you are the queen of prying."

Kelly looked at Erica accusingly. "You told her something, didn't you?"

"I had to," Erica said wounded. "She kept badgering me, and digging and digging. She threatened to go to Theo and ask him what was wrong."

Kelly gasped, "Mom, if something is wrong you come to your offspring first!"

Lola smiled, "I would get nothing from you, you are secretive and you bottle up everything inside. I had to use some strong arm tactics to get Erica to talk."

"Does Dad know?" Kelly asked looking frightened.

"Of course," Lola shrugged, "I can't hide things from your father, especially when this concerns his grandson."

Kelly hung her head. "Now the whole world knows." She raised her hand in the air. "My family, Chris' family, the whole world!"

Lola got up. "I was shocked when I heard. The news was unexpected, I knew you were unhappy but not that unhappy as to go outside of your marriage for solace." She shrugged. "This whole situation takes on special significance when you consider that your husband is the spiritual leader of the church."

"I am never talking to Erica again," Kelly said looking at her sister vengefully.

Lola shook her head, "Open up your eyes Kelly. Erica is not the issue; she is the easiest person to blame right now. What you need to ask yourself is: can I live with this lie hanging over my marriage?"

Kelly nodded. "I can. Hundreds of women do it every day. I realize my mistake, I am sorry both to my husband and to God. I can live with this."

"You will give yourself an ulcer," Lola said exasperated. "Your husband will eventually realize that something is wrong. You have several persons knowing the truth and an ex-lover who is interested in his child. Tell him Kelly!"

"No," Kelly said getting up. "He'll never find out! Chris' family won't tell and neither will you."

"Suppose one day he needs blood and his father finds out he is not compatible," Erica asked.

Kelly turned to her. "Shut up, traitor!"

"Better a traitor than a liar," Erica retorted and clamped her hand over her mouth instantly.

Lola looked at both of them sadly, "I am going to bathe my grandchild. Are you staying for dinner?"

Kelly nodded. "Might as well. What did Maisie fix?" Maisie was the helper and cook.

"I think she did curried goat. She also did a chocolate cake. Erica told her she was spending the night and begged her to do it."

"Sounds good," Kelly said turning to Erica. "I can't stand you."

"Feelings mutual," Erica said, then added, "I made a soap for you today, it has a nice vanilla scent."

"Oh thanks," Kelly said. They never held grudges against each other, and bad feelings never lasted. "I went to Wendy's today and saw Chris."

"Wow." Erica clapped her hand. "Give me the juicy details,

and don't leave anything out."

Chapter Thirteen

"So where've you been?" Kelly looked up from her book and glanced at the clock. She had left her mother's house after a delicious dinner and had put the baby to sleep hours ago.

"You wouldn't believe the night I just had," Theo said, sitting and throwing his keys on the center table. "After the community meeting, which was very productive by the way, I went to a church council meeting at head office. It was supposed to be routine," Theo said leaning back in his chair and rubbing his forehead, "what happened instead was a virtual fist fight."

Kelly gasped. "The clergy acting rowdy! About what?"

"Adultery, divorce, remarriage." Theo closed his eyes.

Kelly stiffened, and was glad that he wasn't looking at her when the word adultery was uttered.

"Apparently," Theo continued, oblivious to her sudden jitteriness, "there is a huge dichotomy between some factions in the council as to what constitutes good grounds for divorce and re-marriage. Bibles were thrown…tempers got heated. It was the clergy version of a bar fight. Remember Reginald from the Little Oaks District?"

Kelly nodded.

"Well his wife went to the US three years ago and decided not to come back to Jamaica. She filed for divorce; it went through and Reginald was left devastated. They had only been married for two years. He has finally met someone new and wants to marry her. The contention is this: his wife—to his knowledge—was not unfaithful and neither was he."

Kelly sat up straighter and gently closed the book she was reading; her hands were trembling. These days she liked to avoid hearing the word adultery at all cost.

"So what do you think about it?" Her voice was tremulous so she cleared her throat in case Theo thought something was wrong.

Theo shrugged, "Jesus himself gave the clause… only if there is marital unfaithfulness—caused by sexual immorality—is there even room to think about remarrying."

"So what is classified as sexual immorality?" Kelly clasped her knees together because they felt a little nervy. It wasn't as if she hadn't heard all of this before. She had even read it in the Bible for herself, but now the whole situation was quite close to home.

Theo sighed. "Fornication, prostitution, adultery."

"So what is Reginald to do? He is young, and it was his wife who divorced him. What is he supposed to do?"

Theo massaged his temples. "I was on his side. The innocent party should be able to remarry. After all he did not instigate or seek a dissolution of his marriage. Some of the older pastors were up in arms though. They said it would send a wrong message to the congregation. Pastor Flanagan threw his Bible at Pastor Henny and the council ended in an uproar."

Kelly stifled a giggle. "Pastor Flanagan is always a passionate guy. Whose side was he on?"

"Apparently not the Bible's." Theo chuckled. "He flung it at Henny so hard that you could hear it thud against his chest."

"And to think you all look so decent on Sabbaths, tut tut tut." Kelly got up and stretched. "I am going to make some tea, want some?"

"Sure." Theo got up too. "I will come with you."

"Remember when we used to do this all the time, stay up late and chat?"

Theo nodded, "I remember. When you have children and demanding jobs suddenly life is not nearly as idyllic as it used to be."

"True." Kelly headed for the cabinet. "Do you want sorrel, ginger tea, or cerrassee?"

"Sorrel." Theo took his seat by the counter.

"I am quite looking forward to Music Day this Sabbath," Theo said as she leaned up against the counter. "I'll be playing one piece on the organ for the church choir."

Kelly nodded.

"That used to be Chris' job but these days I can barely get hold of him on the telephone or anything. When last have you heard from him?" Theo asked her innocently.

Kelly straightened up. What a nasty coincidence? She had just seen Chris today, and had lunch with him. Her lies to Theo were adding up and looming in her mind's eye and she was tired of it, tired of lying.

"I saw him in Kingston today." She turned when she heard the kettle whistling. When she turned back around Theo was looking at her thoughtfully. "Is he involved with anyone?"

Kelly nodded. "That girl we saw him with at the restaurant." She put the tea bag in the hot water and put it before Theo.

The tea was slowly turning red and Theo looked down into its depths. "Her name is Estelle or was it Estella?" He looked back up at Kelly, a serious expression on his face. "I am happy he is moving on."

"Moving on from what?" Kelly grabbed her mug, not registering how hot it was, and how odd she was behaving.

"Moving on from you." Theo stirred his tea and looked at her quizzically. "My mother said something the other day and it has been on my mind."

"Oh." Kelly's fingers were burning up but she still clutched the mug.

"She said that…"

The phone rang and Kelly exhaled; she had no idea she had been holding her breath until the reprieve was granted to her.

"That must be your mother," Kelly said, looking at the phone gratefully. "She had gone to a comedic stage production earlier in the evening."

Theo got up and answered it.

"Tell her goodnight for me honey. I am going to bed." Kelly left the untouched tea on the counter and hurried to the room. Her heart was racing and she realized two things all at once: she couldn't live like this, and her only alternative was to tell her husband, but she just could not.

She pretended to be sleeping when he came in. Theo lay down on his back staring at the ceiling.

Chapter Fourteen

It was barely nine-thirty and the church parking lot was already full. Chris gritted his teeth and wondered if he was going crazy. In an effort to prove to himself, his family, and friends that he was normal and happy he had started going out with Estella.

He looked at her from the corner of his eye and again wondered why on earth he was punishing himself with her. She had insisted that they attend the Three Rivers Music Day. He had refused at first but she had gone on and on about it. She wanted to know why he had left the eldership of the church in the first place, and like a seasoned detective she was under his skin about his reasons. In a bid to shut her up he had shrugged and said it was no big deal—then he had promised to take her to the church's music day.

He realized his mistake when they were at the church. A moment of relief swept over him when he realized that there was no available parking. That was a legitimate excuse, if

ever he was looking for one. He was just about to tell her
so when a car backed out of a spot and left him with no
recourse but to take it. He grimaced and looked over at a
smiling Estella. She had her hair in an elegant upsweep and
was wearing a yellow and black dress that complimented her
slim figure quite well.

She was a pretty girl, he grudgingly admitted to himself,
but for some reason his interest in her had waned after two
days. She was demanding and prone to throw a tantrum if she
didn't get what she wanted; it was a very unattractive trait
in a woman of twenty-five, he thought. Without knowing
much about her family he had concluded that she was an
only child who was indulged by her parents. He had been
pretty accurate in drawing that conclusion, and now, after
three long months of Estella, he just wanted to escape her
clutches.

"You are frowning at me." Estella peered into the pocket
mirror above her seat and smiled. "What's wrong?"

"Nothing." Chris relaxed his facial muscles in the
semblance of a smile. "Just thinking."

"This church is in such a pretty spot," Estella said, changing
the conversation. She had a pretty good idea that Chris was
not pleased that she had bulldozed him into coming to this
particular church, but she badly wanted to go to the music
day and she had felt Chris' withdrawal of affection since the
night they had seen the pastor and his wife at the restaurant—
she knew she had to do something.

Chris had not been able to take his eyes from the pastor's
wife and she wanted to know what was going on. She had
been running around trying to get back the initial attention
that Chris had shown her, but now she was at her wits end.

Added to that he was reluctant to talk about anything
that had to do with this church. Why did a man give up his

eldership in church, except for some major issue? She was dying to know what that issue was and she believed that she was in the right place to get that information.

"Elder Chris." A young woman ran toward Chris when he stepped out of his car and eventually a group surrounded him, gushing about how they missed him.

Estella stood by patiently while they fawned over him and then a woman in pink caught her attention. She was locking up her car and there was an older woman standing beside her with a baby. Two other children had jumped out of the back seat and were heading toward the back of the church, where the children's division was located.

"Don't run," the lady in pink said and the two children slowed down and then quickly walked into church. Estella smiled at their apparent annoyance at their mother for curtailing their fun, and was still smiling when the lady turned around.

It was the pastor's wife. Her curly natural hair was combed into an elegant topknot. When she last saw her she had it down and had been acting pretty strange when she saw her with Chris. Estella stopped smiling when she remembered that and looked at her thoroughly. She was laughing at something that the older woman had said—her honey brown skin was a nice compliment to the pink dress.

Estella had no idea what alerted her to the fact that she was being watched, but she looked up and stared right at Estella and then her gaze swiveled to Chris—in her face Estella could read panic.

What on earth was she panicking about?

Estella glanced at Chris. He was talking to an elderly church sister with his head bent toward her mouth. She could see that he was struggling to leave the clutches of the lady, who had one hand clutching his jacket.

They really love him here. Estella again glanced at the pastor's wife in time to see her hurrying the older woman toward the church. She was in such a hurry that she dropped the toy that was in her hand and had to pause to pick it up.

The older lady stopped almost beside Estella and said good morning, her face friendly and smiling.

Estella looked at her and smiled back.

"Good morning, what a lovely baby." She looked at the baby and then looked at him again, and like a bulb had exploded in her head, she suddenly knew the reason Chris was no longer an elder at the church.

The lady moved on when the pastor's wife picked up the toy but not before Chris looked up and his gaze locked onto her. The tension in the air sizzled even from where Estella was standing.

*****

Chris finally pulled himself away from Sister Plummer. She had declared that she missed him because there was no one in the entire church to listen to her long list of medical issues. He had a fondness for the old lady so he had patiently stood and listened to her list of woes.

In part he was deliberately stalling going into church and in part he enjoyed that Estella was standing their impatiently waiting on him, but Kelly had arrived and the whole scenario changed.

Chris looked at Kelly, but she barely acknowledged him or Estella, she just rushed off into the church as if all the forces of hell were lapping at her feet. He sighed and looked up to find Estella looking at him with a knowing smirk across her face.

He approached her slowly, straightening his tie as he

walked.

"Ready to go inside?"

Estella nodded pursing her lips.

She started to walk beside him then halted. "I think I know the big secret," she blurted out.

Chris looked around, people were heading toward them and he just did not want a show down in the church yard, but Estella had that stubborn look on her face that she got when she was about to throw a tantrum, so he swallowed his impatience and stopped. "The big secret?"

"I am sure of it," Estella nodded. "You and the pastor's wife had a relationship of some sort, didn't you?"

Chris could see the Holmes family approaching, and he did not want them to overhear the conversation so he waved to Ronald and smiled. The patriarch of the family smiled back and came toward him and Estella.

"I miss you around here man." He hugged Chris and guffawed. "But I can see why you are so scarce around the place." He indicated to Estella, who was giving him a pained smile.

"Ah, Ronald," Chris smiled back, both in relief that he had stalled Estella and out of genuine happiness to see his friend. "This is Estella from Great Pond church."

"How do you do?" Estella shook Ronald's hand.

Chris walked beside Ronald as they entered the church foyer talking and laughing.

Estella reluctantly walked behind, pouting all the way.

Theo was in the foyer consulting with two young people and when Chris walked in a small crowd gathered around him just as they did in the parking lot.

Estella fumed inside. He still had the 'hots' for the pastor's wife, she was sure of that, and she was almost sure that the baby was his.

Why else would the pastor's wife be acting so jumpy? She appeared almost scared just now, as if she had something to hide, and the two times she had seen her and Chris in the same vicinity they both acted as if they were guilty–and that baby! That baby resembled Chris, not only in complexion, or the fact that they had the same color eyes, but it could be seen that they had the same shape nose, and mouth as well.

She wondered if the pastor knew. She looked over at him talking and laughing animatedly with a young man at the door. She approached the pastor, a vengeful smile flirting on her lips.

Nobody was going to treat her as second best, she reasoned, and to Chris she was second best. He obviously was still involved with the pastor's wife.

He was crazy if he thought that she would stand for his aloof behavior and treating her as if she was a spoilt child.

"Hello, Pastor Theo," she said, moving towards Theo and the young man.

"Oh hello," Theo broke off his conversation with the young man and gave her a smile. He is so handsome she thought silently. What did that woman have that made her so irresistible to Chris and Theo?

She held out her hand and Theo took it. "You are Chris' friend, Estelle or is it Estella."

"Estella," she smiled warmly at him, "I was wondering, can I schedule a counseling session with you?"

Theo frowned. "You mean alone, without Chris."

Estella nodded.

"That's a bit unusual," Theo said. "When a couple is getting married I normally see them both."

She laughed. "No, it's nothing to do with marriage. It has to do with a little problem I am having—spiritual in nature. I just want a listening ear and some guidance."

"Okay," Theo nodded. "How urgent is it?"

"Very urgent," Estella said. "I was wondering, would tomorrow be okay, maybe in the evening?"

"Okay, I will have to write that down." Theo patted his jacket pocket, and finding no pen turned to the young man next to him, "Floyd do you have a pen?"

"Sure," Floyd gave him a pen and he wrote down the name, Estella.

"Pardon me, Estella. What is your last name and what time would you like to meet? I am free in the afternoon, between three and six, any more time out of my Sunday and my wife will have a fit."

Estella gave him a half smile. "Three is fine."

"Okay," he said, scribbling that on the paper. "Three it is, right here in my office. See you then."

"Okay, have a great Sabbath," Estella said, heading for Chris who hadn't even noticed that she wasn't around.

I am going to punish you, for your lack of attention, she silently vowed to herself as she stood waiting for him, a lonely figure in the church lobby.

Chapter Fifteen

"**I** have a counseling session in fifteen minutes," Theo said to Kelly. He was leaning on the doorjamb to the back verandah.

"Huh?" Kelly's mind had been far away, most precisely at yesterday's music day. She was combing Thealyn's hair and was barely listening to her prattle. Her mother-in-law had been giving her funny looks all day and had disappeared somewhere in the house with Matthew and the baby.

"You seem as if you were far away," Theo gave her a half smile. "Want to talk about it."

"No," Kelly shook her head, "I was just thinking about yesterday."

Theo nodded. "Music day was very spiritual this year, was it not? I'm happy Sister Fawcett carried her mini orchestra. That violin music was really soothing."

Kelly nodded and smiled. "I knew you would like the violins."

"Want to do something when I get back?" Theo asked, looking at his watch. "This is supposed to be a routine counseling session."

Kelly nodded. "Sure."

"Can we go to the Dolphin Park, Daddy?" Thea asked under the cloud of hair that her mother was combing.

"I am not sure," Theo said glancing at his watch again, "might be by the time I get back it will be too near to closing hours. I'll think of something. All right then, in a few."

"Bye daddy," Thealyn said sweetly.

"Bye honey," he kissed Kelly on the cheek and then headed to the garage. His mind was gnawing at him all the way to his church office. Since yesterday there was a certain tension in the air at his house—his mother was decidedly colder toward Kelly and Kelly was unusually silent.

Kelly was acting especially subdued too, as if she was constantly thinking. Her smiles were forced and responses slow in coming, as if she wasn't really aware of what was going on.

Maybe he should have tried to resolve the matter from this morning but he had been intervening in a brewing domestic dispute with a newly baptized couple. The back and forth between the two had kept him out longer than he had anticipated. His parting shot to them—after prayer—had been to remind them that it was only because of the hardness of their heart that they didn't want to forgive each other. That had sunk in a bit and he had seen a distinct semi-frosting of attitudes after.

Sometimes he loved his job dearly but these last few days he was getting a strong impression that he needed to give his family more attention than he was. He wondered if his mother had said something to Kelly about the baby and that was the root of the tension; it was a topic that had made him upset as well. Probably Kelly was searching for a way to tell him that she resented what his mother said.

He pulled into the church parking lot, mulling over his current situation. Usually before a counseling a session he was not so caught up in his own situation. He made a valiant effort to push it to the back of his mind and said a word of prayer before heading into his office.

Two church deaconesses waved at him as he headed around to his office; he waved back. There had been a wedding at the church earlier that morning and they were cleaning it to get it back to a spic and span condition.

Estella was leaning on the wall, waiting for him at the corner of his office. She was in an all black assemble *with* her hair parted in two and slicked back in a fierce bun.

Theo smiled at her. "You look like you mean business Sister Estella." He glanced at his watch. "You are a woman of time, it is exactly three o'clock."

Estella cleared her throat. "The truth is, Pastor Theo, I have been having second thoughts about meeting with you. I've been mulling it over and I was thinking that maybe I am wrong about the whole thing and I should leave it alone."

Theo opened his office door and indicated for her to follow him, he opened up the windows, which overlooked the sea, and let the cool breeze circulate inside the office. The office was quite spacious with a wide desk, a few comfortable chairs, and a mini fridge that was stocked with his favorite cranberry flavored water.

"Would you like a glass of water?" Theo asked Estella, smiling. "Might as well have a drink since you are here already."

"No thanks," Estella said nervously. Theo was looking at her as if she was slightly senile and he had to handle her with care.

She hated when people did that. She clenched her jaw and sat up stiffly in the seat.

He poured water into a glass and then came around to the desk and sat in his chair, it squeaked a little as he sat—Estella sniffed. "The truth is…"

Theo nodded encouragingly, giving her time to articulate her thoughts. She seemed extremely nervous, which wasn't unusual for persons who were coming to him for the first time.

"I was quite alright till I met Chris Donahue," Estella said. "He came to Great Pond church for a few Sabbaths and I got to know him a bit better at a church social event—we had one at our church Saturday night. Before that I thought him aloof and a bit, I don't know—proud?"

Theo nodded sipping his water.

"So we actually hit it off that night, we played dominoes as a team and I realized that he was a down to earth, very nice guy."

"I could tell you that," Theo said smiling.

"It's just that." Estella looked at Theo and then all around the office. "I know for a fact that after we saw you and your wife in that restaurant its like he changed again."

Theo sat up stiffly, his jaw clenching.

"Every time I asked him why he left this church to suddenly visit other churches I was hit by a blank stare and he'd just clam up."

Estella was looking at a stony-faced Theo, who was finding it quite difficult to swallow.

"The other day when I came here, I must admit I got jealous," Estella laughed awkwardly. "They saw each other and again they acted like they were strangers, with her avoiding him, and him giving her intense stares, you know the kind of possessive stare a cat would give a rat before it pounced on it."

Theo could hardly breath he wanted to say something to Estella, anything, but he felt as if his tongue was glued to the roof of his mouth. His fingers were pulsing and shaky.

"Then I saw the baby and I knew what you all are hiding," Estella cleared her throat. "I don't know what kind of cover up business is going on over here, but where I go to church the pastor's wife is above reproach, and she doesn't sleep with the first elder, much less to have his baby. That is wacky. The whole thing is corrupt and sinful and I am not getting mixed up in Chris' sick life, even if he begged me to."

And there it is, laid out bare like fish guts in the sun, Kelly's secret.

Theo could feel all the pressure points on his body pulsing. He had sensed the very things that Estella said, but he hadn't for one moment countenanced those thoughts about his wife. Not one moment. Whenever those thoughts had crossed his mind he had shut them down. Not his Kelly, she'd never do that to him.

He inhaled noisily, his draft of breath the only sound in the room.

Estella was looking at him a startled look in her eye as if she suddenly realized that what she had said to him was something new and devastating.

"Ahm, Pastor Theo, I am sorry," she said hurriedly, "I'm known to vent. I know this is none of my business."

"Sit back down Estella," Theo indicated to the chair, his voice hoarse.

Estella reluctantly sat down. He looked through the window, thoughts running through his head, one upon the other.

In the last year and a half: Kelly ecstatic after working with Chris; Kelly downhearted when pregnant; Kelly fearful when she found out Chris dropped him at the hospital; Kelly and all the world seeing what he should have seen at first— her baby was not his.

His mind listed each point one at a time; he wiped his clammy hands on his jeans and put his head in his hands. He was a cuckolded husband, a fool for not seeing it. He laughed a harsh sound devoid of humor.

Estella jumped when he first erupted in laughter, a guilty voice whispering to her that she should not have said a word.

Theo looked at Estella his eyes slightly wet. "This is not the counseling session I expected," he smiled slightly. "Now I feel as if I need counseling. Have you ever been sucker punched before?"

"No," Estella shook her head, her eyes wide.

"It's not a nice feeling," Theo said and then cleared his throat. "I am going to assume that you came here today to get your revenge on Chris for not loving you as how he loves my wife...Kelly?"

Estella hung her head sadly, "I am so sorry."

"Well, how can I help you now that you have accomplished your mission, the big secret is out. How do you feel?"

"Huh?" Estella stared at him puzzled.

"You exposed them, what's next?"

"I guess...I don't know," Estella was confused.

Theo sighed. "I would say mission accomplished. You punished Chris and with him a whole slew of people, all in one go."

Estella clutched her keys, "I should go."

Theo nodded, he didn't end counseling sessions without prayer but he sat in his office numb. He didn't even watch her walk away; he stared through the window, unseeing until dusk. His thoughts and his body had shut down.

Chapter Sixteen

"Theo," Valda whispered. At first his still figure in the chair had alarmed her to the point that she had been afraid to go around to check to see if he was still alive.

She sighed with relief when he swiveled around, though she could see the blank expression in his eyes and confused look on his face.

"We've been calling you," Valda said whispering, her heart twisting at the pain she saw on his face. "What's wrong? Kelly had one of the deaconesses check that your car was still here. I came over to make sure you are all right. It's seven o'clock you know."

"You were right." Theo's voice was flat. "Kelly's child is not mine."

Valda gasped. "How did you find out?"

"A jealous girlfriend of Chris' came here today under the guise of a counseling session and laid it on thick. I feel punch-drunk."

Valda placed her arms around her son and hugged him tight.

"I am not going home," Theo said forlornly. "I can't face Kelly right now."

Valda's eyes were teary and she rummaged in her purse for a tissue. She dabbed her eye then blew her nose.

"Maybe you could stay with a friend tonight until this blows over and you are more able to deal with this."

"I don't want to deal with this," Theo said throwing up his hand in the air. "Any friend of mine would want to know what's wrong. I'm thinking that enough people already know about this, don't you think?"

Valda sighed. "Maybe you could check into a hotel."

Theo shook his head. "Maybe I should just stay right here."

"Oh Theo," Valda pulled up a chair and sat beside him. He leaned his head on her shoulders. "I have been talking to God about this and asking him for the right way to break it to you, I also asked him to help you through this."

Theo nodded but was staring fixatedly at the wall.

"Oh my baby," Valda said, rubbing his head. "If the devil can mess with families he knows he has a foothold in the church. If he can mess with the spiritual head of the church and his family, he rejoices. It's ironic…" She rubbed Theo's head soothingly. "I used to pray that the Lord protects you from sins of the flesh and so on. I was hearing too many stories of pastors being caught in all kinds of sexual sins, so I placed you before God everyday. I completely overlooked the possibility of your wife being the one at fault. With a false sense of security in your family unity I forgot to pray earnestly for your little family. Maybe if I had done so earnestly enough Kelly would have resisted temptation."

Theo grunted, "I don't want to talk about Kelly, or Chris, or adultery, or paternity tests."

"Okay," Valda sat quietly. Occasionally Theo would get up and pace the room running is hand over his face and sighing heavily. Then he would sit down moving his legs rapidly in a nervous gesture.

After an hour he looked at Valda, his eyes red. "I am going to have to go home."

Valda nodded. "How did you get here?"

"I took Kelly's car."

He nodded and grabbed his key. "Let's go. I need to sleep. I need a clear head."

"Are you sure you want to drive?" Valda asked doubtfully.

Theo nodded. "I am fine. I'll get through this."

Kelly was ironing when they got in.

"Hey," she called out when he poked his head around the laundry room.

"You stopped for service didn't you?"

"Not really," Theo said, trying to avoid looking at her. "I am tired, going to bed."

"Okay," Kelly said, and went back to ironing.

He realized, in a split second, that with his erratic hours these past couple of years and his constant promise breaking, his wife had not even thought it remarkable that he was coming in at that time. To Kelly it was the norm and he found himself going up the stairs heart sore and wondering how much had his attitude contributed to her relationship with Chris?

He slammed down the thoughts about her and Chris, and concentrated on his coping text, Philippians 4:8. *Whatsoever things are true, whatsoever things are honest, whatsoever things are just, whatsoever things are pure, whatsoever things are lovely, whatsoever things are of good report; if there be any virtue, and if there be any praise, think on these things.*

He had been in bad situations before, nothing as shattering as this, but he knew that if he had a knee jerk reaction to this news it would have resounding consequences for the future. This whole situation wasn't just about Kelly's infidelity; children were involved as well.

He stared at the ceiling, listing things that were true, honest and lovely. It suddenly hit him that he had always repeated the text and thought of Kelly, but now she was the antithesis of all these things, especially honesty.

He tossed and turned all night, long after Kelly had come to bed. He wondered spitefully how she could sleep beside him with that big dishonesty weighing on her head and then found that he could not lie down beside her anymore.

He got up at three, went into his study, locked the door and played softly on his piano, 'Burdens Are Lifted at Calvary.' The poignant words reminded him that he was not alone in his heartache and he spent the rest of the night on his knees.

Chapter Seventeen

Kelly watched her husband wearily. He had been acting strangely ever since the music day or was it since he dropped his mother to the airport? He was acting as if he had the cares of the world pressing on his shoulders.

For the past three weeks he hardly spoke to her or looked her in the eyes. He was rarely around. The communication between them was never this bad and she wondered what on earth was eating him. She could barely get a word in edgewise because he used every excuse in the book to get away from her.

He had been lounging in the settee, the Bible opened on his knee.

"I am going out," he said turning to look at her and pocketing his key in his jeans. The baby began to cry and he hesitated before slamming the door on his way out of the house. The noise caused the baby to cry even louder.

Kelly put down the dishcloth she had in her hand and went

to attend to the baby. He was six and a half months old and already he was sitting up in his crib without support. He had a miserable look on his face and was jabbering ba-ba-ba.

It sounded like Dada, something she had pointed out to Theo but he had turned around as soon as he came home and slammed the door so hard, the sound had reverberated through the house.

Was he having an affair?

Kelly sat down in the rocking chair across from the crib with the baby in her lap and rocked him for a while. Thoughts about Theo having an affair ricocheted through her mind and built into a crescendo. The more she rocked the baby the more certain she was that Theo was acting like a man who was seeing someone else.

He barely touched her or talked to her and he wasn't giving her his itinerary as he usually does. Usually she would know exactly where her husband was during the day or what he was doing but since the music day she has been clueless, even just now he just got up, in his casual clothes, and declared vaguely that he was going out. Theo never just announced that he was going out. Usually, he would bombard her with too much information about his whereabouts.

Kelly put back the sleeping baby in the crib and tried to stop her running thoughts. She went onto the veranda and found that she could not stop the thoughts, or the tears.

That's where Theo found her—almost inconsolable—doubled up on the lounge chair at the back of the house. She was sobbing like her heart was broken.

He stood at the door, trying to harden his heart against her but decided that despite everything she was still his Kelly.

He sat beside her on the lounge chair and she looked up, tears streaming down her cheeks.

"Are you hav...having an affair?" Kelly hiccupped.

Theo had tears in his eyes too, "It would hurt, wouldn't it?"

Kelly nodded, "So bad."

He hugged her to him and rubbed her back, "I am not having an affair."

"So why have you been so cold, and where have you been disappearing to?"

"I needed to escape," Theo sighed, twisting himself around so that he could see her face to face.

"Escape from me?" Kelly squeaked.

"Yes," Theo grimaced, "and to pray. I don't think I have prayed so much in the last few years as I have done in these three short weeks."

"Why?" Kelly sniffled, "what did I do?"

"You had an affair with Chris and had his baby and lied to me about it," Theo said matter of factly, all emotion stripped from his voice.

Kelly gasped and struggled to get up from the lounger. "You know? Oh my…I am so…I have to get out of here."

"No you don't," Theo said with a sigh, "sit down."

Kelly stopped struggling and hung her head.

"Look at me Kelly." Theo's voice was tremulous.

Kelly reluctantly raised her eyes to his.

"Is there any other devastating secret lying around that I should know about?"

Kelly shook her head.

Theo sighed. "Have you stopped this affair or is it an ongoing thing?"

"I broke it off before the contract for the villa ended. I am so sorry Theo… I…"

Theo held up his hand, "I know you are sorry. I just want to know things. I have been lied to for so long that I just want to know. Just help me to know." He pleaded.

Kelly nodded.

"Are the other two children mine?"

Kelly gasped, then seeing his tortured expression, said "yes."

"How long have you and Chris had this...this...affair?"

"When I started working on the contract for the villa, I hadn't cheated on you before either," she hurriedly squeezed that in.

Theo looked miserably at her. "How Kelly?"

"How what?" she whispered.

"How will I ever trust you again? Do you even love me, or do you feel a sense of obligation to be with me because we have joint property and children together? Is that why you are here right now?"

"Theo, listen to me, I love you. I am so sorry, I was weak and lonely and ready for someone who gave me the sort of attention that Chris did. I wanted to feel like Kelly, not just mommy or pastor's wife, but desirable, and the center of someone's universe. I have never really felt that I was that important to you. I have always felt that on your list of priorities I was way down somewhere on there with take out the trash."

"Kelly." Theo looked at her pained. "How could you even think that!"

"I am a person too!" Kelly hiccupped. "I may not be as needy as some of your parishioners, but Theo, you must realize that witnessing and nurturing begins at home. I got tired of being reliable Kelly, understanding Kelly or last minute Kelly. I wanted to be precious to somebody. I realize that I was wrong to turn to Chris, I should've shouted loud enough for you to hear about how I felt. By the time I came to my senses, I was pregnant, and I realized without a doubt that you and Thea and Matthew meant the world to me and that I was not only an adulteress, but a deceiver as well. I just did not want to lose my family."

Theo wiped away the tears that were coursing down his cheeks unchecked and stood up, his back hunched. He could barely see in front of him. Every word Kelly spoke was a jab to his heart.

"What about the baby?" Theo turned round to her. "Does Chris know that he has a son?"

Then he closed his eyes, "Of course he does. Everybody knows but me."

"Theo," Kelly pleaded, "I am sorry."

Theo sighed, "Kelly I have looked at this over and over again. For three weeks I mulled it over and over in my mind. I could easily move on from adultery, I know I could, it would be hard but not insurmountable. I could understand your motives somewhat, knowing that you and Chris had a past, but Kelly there is a constant reminder in that house that you lied to me, slept with somebody else and for the love of God Kelly, the older he gets the more he'll look like Chris.

Before long there will be nobody in church who won't be speculating about that boy's paternity, that's if they haven't done so already. The whole situation stinks to high heaven. What would you do if you were me?"

Theo looked at her fiercely. "If I carried a little boy in this house and said, Kelly, here is my son from a church sister, what would you do?"

Kelly hunched her shoulders. "I'd be devastated and humiliated, I'd probably leave."

She closed her eyes, an ache heavy like a fist pressed on her chest.

Theo sat down in a single chair across from her and folded his arms. "I didn't want to make this decision in pain. I wanted to pray about it and have a calmer approach when I finally talked to you about this whole situation."

He sighed and removed an envelope from his pocket. "Two weeks ago when I was at the height of my feverish prayers, I got this in the mail."

He handed it to Kelly and she opened it slowly.

Greetings Pastor Theo Palmer,

We are in the process of recruiting for a chair for our Psychology and Counselling Department at Windsor Christian College. We are aware that you have an MSc in that area and that you have actively practiced counseling as part of your ministry. We would appreciate if you could present yourself as a candidate for this position...

Kelly continued reading and then looked up, "Windsor College? That's in the Cayman Islands."

Theo nodded.

"The pay is certainly more attractive than the one you are now getting as a minister." Kelly handed back the letter to him. "Are you considering it?"

Theo heaved himself out of the chair and began to pace. "Ministry for me has never been about the money. I get a certain satisfaction from spreading God's word and not just preaching it, but living it and showing others to do so. This whole situation with you will derail my efforts in this community for years to come, so this letter was an answer to prayer. I could work in a place where I can start afresh. I know there is no guarantee that I will get the job, but I called in yesterday and confirmed that I was available for a telephone interview tomorrow. If short-listed, I go to Cayman for another interview with the board."

Kelly realized that he said I, and not we, and her heart

gave a little jump. Theo was leaving her, as sure as the sea waves hit the sand far below in the distance her husband was leaving, and it was her fault.

She had managed to break up her family.

She'd be left in a hostile church community that would always be pointing fingers at her as the lady who broke the pastor's heart and broke up her home. The thought was enough to render her speechless.

Theo would leave; maybe send for his children when he was settled. They would want to know why Mommy and Daddy were not living together. Before long they would know the truth and she would be an outcast to her own children when they realized that she was the reason the family was torn apart.

Good job, Kelly, an insidious little voice whispered in her ear, *you managed to mess up your life.*

Chapter Eighteen

After the intense discussion on the back porch, the children had arrived home from school; their chattering had effectively ended the discussion. The word divorce was floating in the air, unspoken but very present in the room.

The baby had cried and Kelly had gone for him, putting him in the playpen in the living room. Theo had sat down across from him, and then, as if on impulse, had taken him out and hugged him tightly. A look of pain convulsed against his features and Kelly had to run to the bathroom to hide her teary swollen eyes from the children.

She left the bathroom with her eyes puffy and red, and headed for the kitchen. The open plan of the living room and kitchen meant that Theo could watch her as she walked toward the counters. He had put the baby back in the pen and was talking to Matthew; Thea was reading to her baby brother while he slapped the pages with his hand and jabbered ba-ba-ba-ba.

The scene was so heart wrenching that Kelly went into the fridge just so that Theo could not see the tears that were pooling at the sides of her eyes. The phone rang and she closed the fridge door and went to answer it.

"Hello," her voice was husky.

"Girl, why do you sound so stuffy. Are you coming down with the flu?"

It was Erica.

Kelly shivered and then started to cry. "He is going to leave me."

She sobbed on the phone as she leaned against the wall weakly. She never heard a word Erica said; she didn't even realize that Theo had taken the phone from her, or that Thea and Matthew were crying as well.

She slumped to the floor, gutted wails escaping her lips. The sheer intensity of her pain meant she could hardly breathe.

Theo tried valiantly to hear what Erica was saying, while around him was pandemonium.

He took the phone out to the patio and closed the door.

"Erica?"

"Yes." Erica sounded like she was sniffling as well.

"It's a tough time." He sighed.

"I know," Erica cleared her throat. "Where are you leaving to?"

"It's not concretized yet, but I am going to do an interview at a school in Cayman."

"Oh," Erica said and then there was silence on the line. "Can't you forgive her?"

Theo rested his head on the wall, "I am working on it… forgiveness is a process. The process for me is just beginning. The pain of it is still very fresh for me. What Kelly did was not just to cheat on me. Honesty, trust, all the things I took for granted in this marriage were smashed…like an elephant walking in a china shop. My new reality is a far cry from the old one. Can you understand that?"

"Yes," Erica said sadly. "I am calling from my parents'. They want to know if they can come over this evening."

"Sure," Theo said. "I won't be here though. I have a meeting with Pastor Henny at six. I need some prayer and counseling and he is my personal pastor and prayer partner."

After he hung up the phone with Erica he went into the kitchen and scooped up Kelly. She was whimpering like a baby, the loud cries were now soft but still gut-wrenching. He placed her on the bed in their bedroom and then he went to calm down the children. By the time he reassured them that Mommy was not dying and that all was well in their world, he gave them supper, feeding the baby with mashed bananas and laughing at his expressions. He really loved this child, and though he was not his, biologically, he was still a part of Kelly and God knows he loved Kelly.

The very thought of living apart from her—or any of his children—made him feel a little fearful inside. There was nobody on the planet who couldn't see this whole scenario from his point of view. He had all right to leave and forge a new life for himself.

Eventually the hurt would ease; he'd find someone new, someone who wouldn't even think of breaking his heart as thoroughly as Kelly had. He'd have another family and he would be able to trust his new wife and she would not lie to him about the paternity of his children.

She would find no other man attractive. She would be his, he would be hers and they'd live happily together until they grew old or until God comes.

The problem with the whole scenario was that in his perfect life his new wife had Kelly's face. Besides, what would happen if he left her alone? Chris would demand visitation rights for his child; they would see each other constantly and start up a relationship again—his children would be Chris' stepchildren.

He'd be the visitor Daddy who jumped ship, he would hardly know them when they grew up and he hated the absentee father relationship with a passion. His father had abandoned his mother when he was little and he had felt it acutely when growing up. He was in a little predicament here. He removed the baby's bib and snuggled him to his chest.

Chapter Nineteen

Kelly slept through her parents' visit. She was so physically and emotionally drained that she vaguely recalled when Theo joined her in bed. She woke up in the morning at around ten o'clock and hauled herself to the kitchen. Erica was reading the day's newspaper around the breakfast table with remnants of her breakfast scattered around her.

"Hey little sister," Erica said, looking up from the paper. "I got your children ready and sent them off to school…made breakfast. I tell you, it was hard to make porridge with the fake milk you guys use, but I persevered…doesn't taste half bad either. Who knew that almond milk was so versatile?"

"Where are Theo and the baby?" Kelly asked, her voice hoarse.

"Theo said he has an interview at nine, and your little munchkin, is at his grandmother's."

"Thank you very much," Kelly whispered. "What type of tea did you make?" she indicated to the teapot.

"Chocolate, of course." Erica giggled. "Chocolate should have its own food group and be placed squarely at the base of the food pyramid."

Kelly rolled her eyes. "Today is your day off?"

"Yup," Erica said perusing the paper. "So I am all yours today. I was thinking, we should go to Gloria's and get a little spa treatment."

Kelly sighed. "I don't deserve to be happy, Erica. I am a cheating, two-timing fool who gave her husband another man's child and lied about it. Now he is leaving me."

"You don't know that yet," Erica said sympathetically, "and with time all this will not seem as sharp. Remember last year when I found out that Jay Jay was already married when he proposed to me?"

Kelly nodded. "That two timing louse. Oh wait, I have no right calling anybody that."

"I felt so dead inside that I thought I would never recover. I saw him at the supermarket last Wednesday evening, and felt nothing. Not one thing. Jay Jay is now just a life lesson."

Kelly nodded. "My life lesson is Mark. My darling son will always be a constant reminder that I was unfaithful. What husband would want that constant reminder around?"

"Maybe you should give him to the Donahue's," Erica said.

Kelly's eyes widened. "No, never!"

"Suppose it comes down to choosing between your husband and your baby, who would you choose?"

Kelly laughed, a humorless sound that echoed in the kitchen. "My husband would never ask me to choose like that."

"But if he did?" Erica asked earnestly.

"I honestly don't know Erica," Kelly shook her head. "Do I sound like the vilest mother on earth?"

They heard the garage door open and close.

"Theo's home," Kelly said, running her fingers through her hair. "I look awful. I guess how I look now will sound the death knell on our marriage. He'll take one look at me and think: boy was I lucky to escape her."

Erica grinned, "You don't look that awful, your eyes are swollen and your nose tip is a bit raw, apart from that you look gorgeous."

"Thanks," Kelly said sarcastically; sipping her tea. "This is good. You must have laced it with sugar."

"Of course," Erica said unrepentant.

Theo came into the kitchen, "Ladies."

"Hey Theo," Erica said brightly.

"Morning," Kelly said.

"I was just offered a job to work in the Cayman Islands as chair of a psychology department at a Christian college. Perks include a relocation package and rent free accommodation in a four bedroom bungalow."

"Congrats," Erica said smiling. "So, did you take the offer?"

"Yes," Theo said, looking at Kelly.

Kelly hung her head and began massaging her temples.

She mumbled, "Excuse me," and got up from the table, her robe snagging in the chair. She grabbed it so hard that it ripped. She left the kitchen once again with tears in her eyes.

"She's taking this extremely hard." Erica watched as her sister drunkenly walked up the stairs as if somebody had hit her on the head.

Theo shrugged, "I clutched the offer with both arms. I want to get away for a while."

"So when are you leaving?" Erica asked curiously.

"A month," Theo said, sighing. "I'll just ship my things over there. I need to be back here in April for Matthew's sixth birthday, June for Thea's birthday."

"And August for Mark's birthday," Erica said softly.

Theo swallowed. "We'll see about that."

Erica sputtered. "You love that child. He is yours in all but biology. You can't just turn off the love."

"I haven't," Theo said sadly, "that is my dilemma."

"Are you going to allow Chris Donahue to move in and take over your family?" Erica asked shrewdly.

Theo groaned. "I should have left them alone from twelve years ago. I should have not gone on that hiking trip. I wouldn't have proposed and they would be together today. Maybe, I am the odd man out in this scenario. Twelve years ago, I forced Kelly to choose between Chris and me. I guess she made her choice this time around."

"Chris is not in the picture, you are making the choice here and now," Erica said. "You are taking yourself out of the equation."

"There should never have been a third person in the equation in the first place," Theo said angrily. "When I married Kelly she became my other half. That is the only equation that should've been; now there's a third party. It makes me sick to think of it.

Believe you me Erica when I tell you that this whole situation has knocked me seriously off kilter. I sometimes think thoughts that I have to subject to God and cry out to him to help me with them. Thoughts about Chris, thoughts about Kelly, thoughts about the two of them having sex, and thoughts about her being so caught up in her little sordid affair that she could be so careless as to get pregnant by him. I have never, in all my life, understood what a crime of passion was until I consider what Kelly has done to me. I have to take a break from her to even begin to feel normal. I have no idea if I will ever be normal again. This betrayal hurts to the core."

Erica nodded, her usually unflappable brother-in-law was hurting, and for the first time since she has known him had she seen this depth of emotion from him. All the cool was gone and in its place was a deeply wounded man. She declined to say a word as he headed out again with a slump to his shoulders.

Chapter Twenty

It was announced on Sabbath that Pastor Palmer would be leaving for the Cayman Islands in four weeks. The news created quite a stir, especially when someone whispered that Sister Kelly and the children were staying in Jamaica until further notice.

"Well, they do have school," Sister Tibbs said wisely. "It wouldn't be prudent to break them from that."

"Did you see how that baby resembles a certain elder who is not worshipping here anymore? And now the pastor is leaving her and the children? Mark my words, you never see smoke without fire," Sister Kym said staunchly.

"The rumor is rife over at another church that Elder Chris was having an affair with Sister Kelly," Sister Tanya whispered, "and to think, Erica and I are friends and she didn't breathe a word to me about it."

Phoebe stuck her head in the conversation and looked at the women. "So that's why Chris was so stand offish to me and the other singles here. He prefers them married."

Sister Tibbs chuckled and then sobered up. "Well what can we do? The pastor and the elder have left, only Sister Kelly is here. The poor woman is probably suffering from deep depression. She's left holding the baby, literally."

Hyacinth Donahue listened with a keen ear not letting on that she had heard a word, but as soon as she got home she called Chris.

"You wouldn't believe what's happening!" Hyacinth said urgently down the phone. "The pastor is leaving Jamaica! There is no mention of his wife or children going."

Chris was silent for the longest time, clutching the phone receiver tightly.

"Mom," he sighed, "he's leaving because he knows."

"What!" Hyacinth said breathlessly, "How'd you know that?"

"Could you believe, that Estella called me crying, saying that she told him her suspicions about Kelly's child being mine and that he had looked so devastated and that she was sorry."

"How'd Estella know?" Hyacinth asked confused.

"She put two and two together," Chris said. "After she confessed I haven't spoken to her."

"Okay then." Hyacinth sighed. "So what are you going to do?"

"Nothing," Chris said wearily. "Don't you think I have done enough? I helped to break up a perfectly good family."

"But what about the baby?" Hyacinth said urgently. "He is yours. We should fight for custody of him."

"No!" Chris coughed. "I am leaving the whole situation with Kelly alone. I'm not claiming parental rights. If I do, I will be tied up with Kelly for years, I am trying to move on with my life in a healthy way. Kelly and thoughts of her are unhealthy for me. With her, I am obsessed. She's like a drug to me and I am slowly weaning myself from it. I can't get suckered into her again, Mom."

"But the baby…" Hyacinth whispered.

"The baby will have a great father in Theo, if he ever decides to forgive his wife." Chris's voice choked with tears. "I made my peace with the whole thing. I think you guys should too."

When Hyacinth hung up the phone, she let out a long, deep, and heartfelt sigh.

*****

"So are you all packed?" Kelly was standing at the doorway to the room that was once theirs. She had no tears left. They hadn't really talked since he announced to the church that he was leaving, he even broke the news to the children himself without her participation.

He straightened up, "I will bank the household and living expenses in our joint account as usual."

Kelly nodded, biting her lips.

"I wanted to come back for the children's birthdays, but I am not sure if I should, it's too soon to come back, you know…"

Kelly nodded again.

"If you resume your relationship with Chris I would stay in a hotel when I'm here. Don't want to step on another man's territory, though he had no problem trampling all over mine. Maybe then we can rationally discuss the ending of our marriage."

Kelly stammered. "Re…re…resumed, what are you talking about?"

Theo glanced at her, his heart breaking a little. He did a

good job of hiding his pain from Kelly and for the past three and a half weeks he had started sleeping in the spare room, preparing for their separation and missing her like crazy. He hadn't even left the house yet, and already he was sad and painfully lonely.

"You deserve to pursue your first choice, Kelly." Theo spun around and hunched his shoulders. "I am moving out of your way. Maybe you'll make a better property developer's wife than a pastor's wife."

"Stop it," Kelly rasped. "I am not going to be walking off into the sunset with Chris when you leave. What happened between Chris and me is over. I haven't spoken to him in ages. I don't want to resume anything with him. What I want is for my husband to take me with him, flaws and all, and let us work this out together."

She clutched her chest. "Please don't leave me behind, Theo. Please!"

She hugged him from behind, her hand clutching his taut belly. "I am sorry. I am sorry. I am sorry."

She thought she had no tears left but they welled up in her eyes and started to flow again.

Theo turned around and hugged her to him tight. "If only we could step back in time, and heal our hurts...right our wrongs."

"We can." Kelly looked up at him, her eyes shining. "It's called forgiveness. It is our time travel."

Theo wiped away a tear from her face with his thumb. "But there's this thing called consequences, it stares you in the face everyday and with it a real reminder of how devastating the hurt that we cause others can be."

Kelly stepped back. "And in our case, the consequence is Mark?"

Theo didn't answer.

"Do you hate that baby?" Kelly whispered.

"You know I don't," Theo said giving her a look of reproach. "I love him, like I do Matthew and Thea. Up until a couple weeks ago I thought he was mine."

"So just let it go," Kelly said, her voice fading away.

"Remember that song you love so much? 'Ordinary People'"

Kelly nodded.

"I think the lyrics sum up our situation." Theo kissed her on her forehead. "I'll call you when I get there."

Chapter Twenty-One

Theo stood under the "EXIT sign," waiting for one Cynthia Berry from the school to pick him up. He felt a tap on his shoulder and spun around. A petite lady with a wide smile was looking at him.

"Pastor Palmer."

"Yes," Theo nodded.

"I'm Cynthia Berry, your official welcoming committee, tour guide, and driver. Welcome to Grand Cayman."

"Thank you," Theo said, grinning.

"My vehicle is this way." She indicated to a red sports utility vehicle that was parked at the edge of the parking lot. He followed her and stowed his bags in the back of the vehicle.

"We had a little fight to come pick you up," Cynthia said, grinning. "There were so many volunteers to do this one deed."

Theo smiled. "Why is that?"

"Well, we saw your picture." Cynthia was laughing. "Anyway, I won the haggling because I live across from you. Can you imagine that? Don't look so scared." Cynthia looked over at Theo. "I am not a stalker, and I know that you have a wife."

Theo exhaled in relief.

Cynthia laughed as she pulled onto the main road. "Are you hungry? We could stop and get a bite to eat."

"Sure!" Theo said. "I wasn't hungry when I left Jamaica, but now I'm famished."

Cynthia nodded, "I am sure that Hilma…the housekeeper that the three houses in our cul-de-sac share…cooked up a storm for you. In any case, it would be nice to eat at 'Breezes by The Bay.' It will give you a good intro to our island."

"Sounds good," Theo said, basking in the atmosphere of Cayman and enjoying the sea breeze he felt through the car window.

When he had stepped out of the plane he thought that he would feel lighter somehow, now that he had put some much needed distance between him and Kelly, but instead he felt a tug of loneliness so intense he had to struggle to breathe.

That sense of loneliness was accompanied with a sense of betrayal that instantly made him feel angry.

He should have been arriving in Cayman with Kelly and the children. It would have been like an adventure. His contract with the school was a two-year one and he wondered what was he going to do with himself when it was over, and what would be the state of his marriage?

The question made him grit his teeth and he barely heard when Cynthia breathlessly said, "here we are."

He looked outside and realized that they were at a building that overlooked the water.

"One of the best eateries downtown," Cynthia declared.

"Ah," he said getting out of the car and looking out at the frothy blue sea. "I love the view."

Cynthia laughed. "Cayman has a view from almost everywhere. Where we live, on the East Side, the water is spectacular. You wake up to bird-songs and fall asleep to the lullaby of the sea. The school is not far from where we are now, but first things first. Let's eat and then I'll show you around."

They ordered fish and chips and sat looking out at the bay—a calming sight that reminded him of home in St. Ann, and with it, bittersweet memories.

Cynthia was looking at him, feeling a bit tongue-tied. He was truly gorgeous and she was not kidding when she told him that they had practically fought in the teachers' lounge for the pleasure of picking him up from the airport.

"So tell me about the school." He looked at her with his warm brown eyes and she stared at him for so long he was starting to feel concerned.

"I am sorry," Cynthia said, hurriedly sipping her drink. "I think I have just a teeny bit of a crush on you."

Theo grinned. "You are very honest."

"I know," Cynthia sighed dramatically. "I have no guile or tact or diplomacy. Honesty dogs my feet wherever I walk. Hence, the reason I am single."

Theo laughed. Other diners were looking at him, but he didn't care. For the first time in weeks he could laugh about something.

His mood lifted a bit after that, and he gave Cynthia the sternest expression he could muster. "Cynthia honesty is a fruit of the spirit, it's a gift. It was Thomas Jefferson who said that honesty is the first chapter in the book of wisdom. So tell me about the school, and where I'll live…everything."

She grinned with him. "Well, as you can see, Cayman is

beautiful. The school is on the outskirts of this town, not far from here. The house is on the East End, where life is a little slower than the West End, with its high-rise buildings and commerce. Our school enrolls a total of 800 students. Our department has a total of 115 students."

"So you are in Psychology too?" Theo asked Cynthia, cupping his chin.

"Yes sirree," Cynthia grinned. "I'm an adjunct lecturer, which makes you, as department chair, my boss."

"So are you from around here?" Theo asked, realizing for the first time that he had not really looked at Cynthia. She was a very attractive woman. She had whisky brown eyes, thick well-shaped eyebrows and a pink bow of a mouth that looked like it was permanently turned up in a smile.

"Yes, I am," Cynthia said. "I'm a native Caymanian. My parents reside in Miami now but I was born here, so the moment a lecturer position opened I came back home."

Theo nodded.

"So can I ask you the question I've been burning to ask?" Cynthia said nervously.

Theo raised his eyebrows and then half smiled. "She is back home in Jamaica with the children. I have no idea if she will be joining me out here."

Cynthia grinned. "I wasn't the only one wondering. We were all wondering when your family would join you."

Theo sighed. "I have no definite answer."

Cynthia was burning to ask if everything was all right with their relationship. He wasn't even wearing a wedding band. Was that a sign that he's separated? She bit off the burning question at the tip of her tongue. She would suppress her questioning for now.

Theo entered the bungalow after Cynthia left. A lady

named Hilma, who was supposed to be his housekeeper on Mondays and Wednesdays, informed him that the house was in tip-top shape.

A car was in the garage for him to use for the duration of his stay and the fridge was stocked. He would report to the college tomorrow and learn more about his position. Cynthia had invited him to a barbeque with other staff members and friends at her house, which was just across the road from him, hidden behind thick flowering bougainvilleas. He had refused. He was too tired—in body and spirit—to contemplate being social right now.

He looked around the house. It was at the very end of the cul-de-sac with three other houses; it had manicured lawns and mature fruit trees. The design was Mediterranean; had a deep burnt orange color and the windows and doors had mosquito screens.

The rooms were spacious and he headed to what looked like the master, throwing himself across on the queen-sized bed. He closed his eyes and listened to the sea, which was a few feet below the back deck.

It's lovely here, and so peaceful. He heard his cell phone ringing and reluctantly answered it. He knew it was Kelly. He had promised to call when he arrived. He looked at his watch; it was eight o'clock. Hearing her voice would shatter his peace-of-mind.

"Hey." He answered the phone drowsily.

"So you reached safely." She sounded relieved. "We were getting worried."

"Sorry I didn't call." He took off his shoes. "I went for a bite-to-eat with Cynthia, my welcome-to-Cayman person."

"Oh?" Kelly said, hoping that he would elaborate.

Theo, hearing the curiosity in her voice, decided not to tell her anything more. In the past he would have rattled off details; reporting faithfully like her little puppy, but he felt as if that part of him was broken or hiding in anger, pain, and betrayal. He had no reason to reassure her. She had broken the trust in their relationship and the monumental task of putting it back together was beyond him right now.

"Can I speak to Matthew and Thea?" he asked her in the silence.

"Sure, sure," Kelly stammered.

She called the kids, and he closed his eyes as a shaft of pain grazed his heart.

After talking to the children, he didn't ask to speak to Kelly again; he couldn't handle hearing her anymore. The icy control that had encased his reactions to her devastating news was slowly melting, and he felt a surge of anger toward her so powerful he squeezed his eyes shut and weathered its onslaught.

Chapter Twenty-Two

Kelly drove into the church parking lot; she had the music on very low. It was one of her favorite classical pieces. The children were bickering in the back and occasionally she had to intervene. She had to take them to choir practice, but her mother would pick them up later and keep them.

She needed the break; she could see herself slithering on the knife-edge of a breakdown. Theo was now gone for two weeks and already she was feeling the stress of single parenthood.

She hated it. It made every paltry excuse she made in the past about Theo not being around and not supporting her seem like a wimpy lie. At least when he was around she had help with the children. They usually listened to their father and were happy.

Now she was dealing with two children who seemed to thrive on driving her crazy—the constant questioning about Daddy and when he was coming back was driving her nuts.

The church people were acting all funny as well. Conversations stopped when she came near and the little whisperings and long looks especially at the baby indicated to her that they all knew or suspected. No one had actually come out and said anything, but she knew that they knew and were judging her. The accusatory looks of the elders and senior church leaders were a very big indication of that.

She wished that she wasn't the one left behind. She parked beside a car that looked like Chris' and her heart lurched a bit but she quickly composed herself and turned to her two bickering brats.

"Now listen to me," she said, looking at Thea sternly. "You are the older one; you should be setting an example for your brother. You two behave yourself at practice and behave yourself at Grandma's."

They mumbled.

"What was that?" Kelly asked sternly.

"Yes, Mommy," they said in unison.

"Okay, your grandma will be here at seven to pick you up. I will come and get you guys tomorrow in the evening."

"Are you going to leave us, like Daddy?" Matthew asked earnestly, tears pooled in his eyes.

"No, no, none of that," Kelly said impatiently. Matthew had been melancholy ever since Theo left, and nothing she said would convince him that their father had not abandoned them, even though he spoke to them every night.

She stared into empty space long after they went into the church and then closed her eyes. It was her fault they were not all together right now.

She knew it and it seemed as if they did too, turning hurt eyes in her direction whenever they asked her when their Daddy was coming home and she couldn't tell them anything.

How was she to know? Theo had effectively left them

to their own devices and he sounded like he was enjoying himself in Grand Cayman.

She winced. He even sounded as if he had found somebody else. He was always mentioning this Cynthia person, and she was sure he liked her. The thought made her shudder. The thought of Theo having somebody else in his life was always enough to make her weak with fear. The irony did not escape her though. She slumped over the steering wheel, willing herself to drive out of the parking lot.

The knock on her window made her jump, and she gasped when she saw Chris. He was grinning at her.

"Are you stalking me, Kelly?"

"Nooo!" Kelly said breathlessly. "What are you doing here?"

"Tonight is the new pastor's reception party, or whatever they call it."

"Oh, I must have missed that announcement last week," Kelly said vaguely. "I spend most of my time in the mothers' room now anyway. Can't stand the knowing looks, especially from Phoebe and that girl Tanya."

Chris frowned. "You look sick. What are you doing here if it's not for the function?"

"Thanks a lot for the compliment," Kelly grinned. "Sick is the new look this season. I am here because my children have choir practice."

"So are you waiting for them?" Chris asked, "I could keep your company."

"No," Kelly sighed, "I was sitting here willing myself to drive home. I have a slight headache and a big life ache."

"Life ache? That's what I've got too. Want us to swap stories?"

Kelly leaned onto the steering wheel and twisted her head to look at Chris. "My association with you is what is causing my life ache."

"So you guys are separated, huh?" Chris asked, leaning into the window.

"Something like that," Kelly sighed.

"Tell you what," Chris said earnestly. "Follow me up to my house. I know something that might be of some interest to you. It might take your mind off your life ache."

"No!" Kelly groaned. "I am not in a million years going to your house. Have you not heard a word I said? I am suffering because I followed you somewhere in a quiet room one too many times. I am done with that! Not interested."

Chris grinned. Kelly was looking so vulnerable and dreary.

"I won't jump you, I promise. Besides, my sister Camille is staying with me for a week. She has some business to do out here."

"That's your possessive evil sister," Kelly said tiredly. "I cussed her out once. I won't go near her again."

"I got a big contract," Chris said, leaning on the door. "This hotel group wants to buy an old property here in St. Ann's Bay and turn it into an all-inclusive. They have asked if I can recommend an interior decorator after their renovation is completed. Instantly I thought of you, but I had vowed to keep out of your way so…"

Kelly scrambled out of the car angrily and looked at Chris. "Do you realize that this was how we first got involved? You dangled work in front of my face, and I snapped it up like a greedy pig. If I hadn't done your villa, I would still be with my husband, whom I love dearly. I love him. I wish I hadn't taken that job."

Tears sprang to her eyes. "My whole life is wrecked. I am a mess. I have no appetite. I barely sleep. No wonder you think I am sick. I hate you Chris! I hate you! She threw up her hand in the air. I really, really hate you!"

She started crying in earnest and didn't even realize that she was sobbing on his shoulders in the middle of the church's parking lot.

"Hush, Kelly," he was saying sympathetically, "I am sorry."

She sobbed until she had no tears left, just a heartbroken feeling in the pit of her stomach that needed to be released. She felt like screaming, and she had to put her hand to her mouth to stop the guttural-wounded sound from escaping.

Chris hurriedly bundled her into the car. He called somebody on his phone and the next thing she knew he was driving her home.

He fumbled for her key in her purse and gently led her to the settee. Kelly slumped onto the settee like a wooden doll.

"I hate my life." Her eyes and nose were swollen and her head was throbbing.

She vaguely heard the phone ringing. Chris was sitting across from her looking at her as if he expected her to do something drastic.

The concern in his eyes almost made her want to cry again. The phone kept ringing and finally Chris said, "I am going to answer it. It could be an emergency. That's about the twentieth ring."

Kelly shrugged; she didn't care who it was. She was so cloaked in misery it actually felt like a physical oppressive presence.

Chris answered the phone and the thought suddenly occurred to Kelly that it might be Theo. Chris stayed away for a while, and when he returned he looked at her cautiously. "That was Theo."

She closed her swollen eyes in defeat. "Someone should just kill me now and get it over with."

Chapter Twenty-Three

Theo sat down on the deck looking out at the sea and thinking about things. These days his thoughts were constantly on Kelly. He couldn't seem to shake his need of Kelly. He knew she had cheated and had another man's baby and that made him angry, but the clarity of thought that he had sought by putting distance between himself and her was not coming.

Maybe he should have stayed and fight it out. He always counseled people to ventilate their issues. Let it all out, don't let it fester and rot and assume larger-than-life proportions. He was doing the same thing that he had warned others against. And what's more, he never really argued with Kelly. He never really told her how he felt.

He had always felt that saying exactly what was on your mind could hurt more than anything else; some relationships never recovered from an argument and he had thought some pretty sick stuff toward Kelly. He had vacillated between wanting to find out exactly what she did with Chris, every minute detail about their affair, and then realized that it would be counter-productive to even hear it. Some things were better not knowing.

He wondered if he would ever get over it. Would he be able to shake this feeling of betrayal?

Could he trust her again?

He didn't know how, but he would try. His marriage was important to him and he knew that not fighting for it would make him a quitter, and he was never one to quit a challenge.

It was that thought that propelled him to enter the house and call Kelly. He had not really talked to her since he left. He had deliberately given her the cold shoulder, as he had wanted her to suffer some. It might have been childish of him, but it made him feel better about the whole thing. She deserved to suffer just as she had made him suffer.

He dialed the number and listened to it ring incessantly. He tried about five times before it was picked up and Chris answered.

At first, Theo was shell-shocked. His head felt as if it had swollen to twice its normal size, and his blood pressure shot up through the roof. He squeezed the phone so hard he was sure that if it was anything else but hard plastic it would have dented.

"It's Theo," he'd said, clearing his throat. Several thoughts were running through his head at the same time and the one that was on the tip of his tongue sprang out. "So have you moved into my house, too? Picked up where you left off with my wife? Having sex in my bed?"

"Hell no," Chris had sighed. "I brought home Kelly. She was crying hysterically in the church parking lot. I didn't think it wise to let her drive in the condition she was in. She is saying that she does not want to live and I am of two minds, should I leave her here…"

"Where are the children?" Theo asked alarmed. His hand had loosened off the phone and his concern for Kelly took over.

"Apparently she had taken them to practice. Kelly said her mother would pick them up. She did mention, before she started screaming 'I hate you' to me that she was not eating or sleeping. She looks sick, like she's on the verge of a nervous breakdown or something."

Theo sighed. "Call Erica; she will stay with her. I can't believe I am saying this, don't leave her there alone."

"Okay," Chris said. "I'll call Erica as soon as we are done talking."

"Okay," Theo said and hung up.

He felt shivery; he got up and started pacing. Their separation was taking its toll on Kelly worse than he thought.

He felt a little tingle of pleasure at the thought of her shouting at Chris that she hated him, but then a more serious thought occurred to him. If Kelly had a nervous breakdown who would take care of his children? He couldn't go back to Jamaica just now—he had just started his job. He paced for an hour and then called Erica.

"Are you at the house yet?"

"Yes," Erica answered, sounding subdued. "I got a friend to prescribe a sedative for her. I had to medicate her; she was hysterical."

Theo winced. "Is Chris still there?"

"No," Erica said. "He's gone to the new pastor's greet-the-church thingy. They called him, to give a speech or something. Apparently the new pastor is his friend."

"I hope he doesn't have sex with the new pastor's wife," Theo said sarcastically, then sighed. "I thought he and Kelly had resumed their affair."

Erica chuckled. "Kelly is in no condition to have an affair

with anyone. She looks like something the cat dragged in. Mom and I will have to work out some form of arrangement for the children. Kelly is in no shape to take care of them right now. She looks like she has practically dissolved since you left."

"Keep me updated on her progress," Theo said. "Tell her I called, will you? I'll call her tomorrow. And thank you, Erica."

He hung up the phone and went back out onto the deck. He could barely see the sea below, but he could hear it. It soothed him somewhat. He silently prayed for Kelly and then for himself.

"Help me Lord, to forgive her."

*****

He was in his office with a sheaf of papers on his desk when Cynthia poked her head around the door.

"Hey, neighbor."

"Hey, Cynthia," he said, smiling at her. She was always asking him out and he always rejected her advances. He didn't want to encourage her, but she had a very effective strategy to make him laugh.

"Has anybody asked you to go to the faculty social yet?"

He shook his head. "No."

"So do you want to go with me, as my date?"

"Er...date?" Theo looked at her askance. "You do remember that I am not single, don't you?"

Cynthia came into the office fully. "Yes I do, but I was hoping that you would confess to me first, not anyone else, that you were on the verge of divorce. I could comfort you. Purely platonic comfort, of course."

Theo looked at her contemplatively. "Have a seat please."

"Ooh, this sounds serious," Cynthia sat down warily.

"Cynthia, you are a riot," he said, relaxing in his chair. "My wife's name is Kelly."

Cynthia nodded.

"She freelances as an interior designer. Our children are still in school. Hopefully they will be here with me in the summer. She is not well at the moment, and I think a part of her problem is that we parted ways several weeks ago with some yet to be resolved marital issues…I think she misses me a lot. The thing is, I miss her too." He gave Cynthia a half smile. "If I come to the faculty social it can't be as your date."

Cynthia sighed. "I was so hoping you were getting a divorce." Then she clasped her hand over her mouth. "Sorry, I am so sorry. It's just that you aren't wearing a ring, and we all thought your wife was a doozy for letting you come over here alone, seeing as though you are so fine and all."

Theo laughed. "Your honesty is as usual quite refreshing."

He called Kelly after Cynthia left the office; he had not wanted to call her when he got in from his morning run since it was too early, he reasoned.

She answered the phone groggily, "Hello."

"Hey, Mrs. Palmer," Theo said solemnly. "I heard that you wanted to die last night. How are you this morning?"

"Theo?" Kelly asked in a hoarse voice. "Are you still talking to me?"

"Yes," Theo said. "Why wouldn't I?"

"Because Chris answered the phone last night and because I am the worse person on the planet," she coughed, "lower than the dirt on your shoe."

Theo grinned. "I really don't think you are lower than the dirt on my shoe, Kelly. You are the mother of my children. I consider you a lot higher than that. Chris explained why he was at the house, and told me that you hated him. That made me feel especially good."

Kelly sneezed. "I am stupid though, threw away my relationship with you and broke up my family." She sniffled. "I don't even pray anymore. Why would God listen to me, an adulteress?"

Theo paused. "Kelly, now is the time to pray. God is faithful and just to forgive you of your sins however bad they may seem in your eyes. Lay your burdens at his feet and let him deal with it for you. No wonder you are so down and depressed. Are you sorry for what happened? Genuinely sorry? Not just sorry because I found out."

"Of course." Kelly sniffed. "I was very weighed down with my deception. I contemplated confessing to you so many times I could not count. I got cold feet every time. I just wanted things to be normal again. I wished so many times that I could just press undo and wipe my slate clean. I am genuinely sorry, not lip service sorry. Really sorry… running myself crazy sorry."

"Okay I hear you," Theo said contemplatively. He could sense her earnestness and it struck a chord within him. "Would you do it again though, have an affair or strike up a relationship with Chris? Have you really gotten over him, Kelly? Has he gotten over you?"

"I am very much over Chris," Kelly said, clearing her throat. "I think he was my first real crush. I was dizzy when I was around him back in the days. Those were young idyllic days. I was suffering from nostalgia when I had that affair with him."

"Unfinished business," Theo suggested a shaft of pain, striking him suddenly. "You two never had sex when you were dating, and you just had to try him out, no matter the cost."

"No it wasn't like that," Kelly sneezed, "I was lonely…"

"I am not taking responsibility for your affair," Theo bit out. "I am lonely now. I am in a foreign country without my family, not because I want to be but because you caused it, would I be justified in having an affair? How would you feel if I had one?"

Kelly was silent.

Theo inhaled. "I am willing to forgive Kelly, but I am a man. We both need to talk to God about the situation. Don't forget, He listens. He is the only way we are going to get past this."

Kelly sneezed again. "I am happy that we could talk, and I am more than grateful that you are willing to forgive me."

Theo was silent for a long while. "I love you, I really do. Refusing to forgive you would hurt me too. I just need time."

Kelly murmured, "Thank you for that, Theo. I love you too."

Chapter Twenty-Four

Over the next few months Theo worked out a routine. He spoke to Kelly every morning, and they started praying together again, something they hadn't done in years. She called their morning sessions her counseling sessions. He went to work and at midday he would call her again. In the evenings, he carried the phone onto the deck, stared up at the stars, and talked to her about everything and nothing.

It was close to April 25th, Matthew's birthday. He hadn't seen them for four months and he was genuinely missing all three children.

Gradually he made peace with the fact that Mark was not his biological child, but he was a part of Kelly and that was something he was just going to have to live with if he reconciled with her. And he was going to reconcile with her. He could barely get by without hearing her voice. They were acting as if they were just dating each other; she loved to hear about every little detail of his day, and he couldn't get enough of her voice whenever she described anything to him.

March turned into April, and he flew to Jamaica for Matthew's birthday. Kelly was the best sight he had seen for months, when he saw her at the airport waiting for him. She ran and leapt into his arms. He held her for so long that people were staring at them and smiling.

"You are a sight for sore eyes," he whispered in her ears.

"You too." She looked him over. "You look more muscular."

"Jog and lift weights every morning, and at night so that after talking to you I can fall into bed exhausted."

"Are you still dodging, Cynthia?" Kelly asked, laughing.

"Of course." Theo held her hand and they walked to the car together. "She is severely honest about her feelings for me."

Kelly laughed. "I should show up and shock her."

Then she stopped and silently looked at him. She had been waiting for him to invite her and the kids to move to Cayman. She even found herself packing little things and thinking of the move, but as yet they hadn't talked about her living with him again.

She missed him so badly these past few months that she could taste it.

He ignored her statement and got into the car. "I missed driving you," he said to the car.

She got in and said brightly, "How was your trip?"

"Short," he said abruptly and then repented silently when he saw the pain on her face.

"I am looking forward to this weekend though," he said, changing the topic. "I can't believe your mother volunteered to have the party at her place. Has she forgotten about last year when we had it at our house with little five and six year olds swarming the place and yelling at the top of their lungs?"

Kelly laughed. "She volunteered. I could not say no."

They talked all the way home and he went into the house, a feeling of nostalgia hitting him hard. His family was here— what was he doing in Cayman alone? But a cautious voice told him to tread softly. He was still smarting a bit from the wound that Kelly had dealt him. There was no reason to rush anything. He headed to the spare room and dropped his bag on the bed.

Kelly stood at the doorway; she had followed him up the stairs.

"I cooked your favorite dinner."

He smiled. "Curried garbanzo beans. I haven't had that in a while."

She smiled, but the smile did not reach her eyes. She looked at the bag on the bed then at him. She cleared her throat.

"I thought..." She leaned on the door. "I got the impression...I was thinking...Theo, why are you sleeping in the spare room?" she blurted out.

"We are still taking it slow," Theo said, standing up and kissing her on her nose.

"Okay," Kelly huffed. "We'll see about that," she muttered under her breath.

When Erica dropped off the children, they were so happy to see their father that Kelly had to abandon the conversation with him.

Theo exclaimed about how big Mark had gotten and how he was already teething. He had to use sheer willpower to stifle the regret he felt about not being there to see each stage of his early development.

He had a hard time putting the children to bed; Kelly had totally abandoned him to it. He staggered to the spare room after telling them story after story.

He had resorted to reading First and Second Chronicles to get them to feel sleepy and then he had felt a twinge of guilt that he had used the Bible as a sleeping aid.

When he reached the spare room he found that the door was locked; he tried the lock again.

"Kelly," he whispered to himself, "that imp."

He headed to the master bedroom and saw that she was sprawled off in bed with a skimpy silk nightgown barely covering her torso and a half smile playing across her lips.

"Are you looking for this?" She opened her gown slightly to reveal the key that was nestled between her breasts.

"Kelly," Theo swallowed. "We are taking this slow, remember?"

"Sure," Kelly said, widening her gown further.

Theo approached the bed slowly. "Kelly, a man can only take so much and no more." He sat on the bed and touched her lips.

Then he kissed her. It was a kiss of promise, and it felt like they were kissing for the very first time.

He deepened the kiss and slowly made love to his wife, his love.

Chapter Twenty-Five

Theo had left Jamaica that weekend, very sure that he was over the deepest of the wounds that the affair had caused him. There was still a low humming twinge somewhere in his heart, but he was learning to live with it.

He had not said a word about her and the children moving to live with him in Cayman, and he could feel her disappointment about that, but the weekend was the happiest he had been in years. There was something about almost losing the most important thing in your life to make you appreciative of what you have, and to him he had almost lost Kelly.

He had Thealyn's birthday to attend in four weeks, and the weeks dragged by interminably. He had told everyone that his family would be joining him in August. He thought that would give Kelly enough time to pack up and arrange for the house to be taken care of. He already spoke to the principal of the private school where he wanted the children to be enrolled.

On his second trip to Jamaica, he told Kelly not to pick him up. He had one last thing to do before he could move on fully with his marriage—he had to face Chris. They had to talk about this.

He decided to rent a car. The drive from Montego Bay into Ocho Rios took him past the Villa Rosa. He was grateful when he saw Chris' car in the driveway and he decided to stop. For a second, his imagination ran wild and he wondered about the things that Chris and Kelly used to do right here in this villa.

It took a minute to calm the nausea that came with the thought. When he had composed himself he drove up to the gates and told the security that he was there to see Chris Donahue. The security called the office and the gates were opened for Theo.

The grounds were extremely beautiful with a profusion of roses greeting him at the front of the villa. The flowers lent a subtle sweetness to the air.

He walked into the reception area. The décor was tastefully done and he silently applauded Kelly's handy work. Behind the desk Chris opened a door and gestured for him to follow.

He went into the office, which was surprisingly spacious, and sat down in a chair that Chris had pointed to.

They sat facing each other, and there a stare-down ensued. Theo wondered bitterly, how could Chris sit in a meeting with him and fellow elders when he was screwing his wife? How could he have looked him in the eyes and discussed church plans, all the while knowing what a traitor he was being? Didn't it take a special kind of barefaced sinner to do that? He slammed down that thought firmly; his left eye started to tick.

Chris was the first to look away.

Theo cleared his throat. "I was just passing by, saw your vehicle and impulsively decided to stop. I have not really spoken to you since I found out that you had sex several times with my wife and impregnated her. I was going to call you today actually." He ended the statement politely as if they were casually talking about the weather.

The sound of heels clicking on the marble floor outside ended the silence after Theo's statement.

Chris cleared his throat. "I am sorry you were hurt." He drummed his pen on the table. "I am sorry about the whole thing. I am not going to lie. I have loved Kelly from a distance for years. I wanted to take her from you. I don't know what I was thinking."

"Everybody is sorry. Let's all slap a band aid on it and forget it happened," Theo growled. "To think, Chris, that I encouraged you to talk to me, to tell me about this woman that had you in knots. I was actually feeling sympathy for you, remonstrating with you about women. When all along you were talking about my wife, mine, my wife! I married her; I love her; we have a family. You should have stayed out of it, you should have known better and yet you say you don't know what you were thinking?"

Theo scoffed and threw his hands up in the air. "You were thinking that you had to have Kelly at any cost. You wanted her to turn her back on our children and me and live with you. You struck when she was low and vulnerable and though she should have known better she willingly went along with it."

Chris swallowed. "That's not…"

"Let me finish," Theo bellowed, he stood up and paced. "I have thought about this conversation for months. I have thought about taking your neck in my bare hands and squeezing it till you are lifeless. I have been so angry I would have loved to see you and Kelly rotting in Hell together.

To think that in this very room you two might have even had sex …" his voice trailed off. "But eventually I calmed down. I clung to Jesus so hard during this whole situation that believe it or not, I do not feel as vicious as I once did. I am a man determined to rescue his family from being broken up. Kelly is my family, Chris, and so is the baby. So I have to ask, what are your plans for the baby? I can't live with the thought of you having some attack of conscience later on in life and deciding to claim Mark. I do not want you anywhere near Kelly or my family ever again."

"I have no plans for Mark," Chris said, heaving a sigh. "I have completely bowed out of the picture." He spread his arms wide. "Kelly made it plain to me sometime ago that you were the love of her life. Last time we talked she said she really, really hates me. I would have liked to have a relationship with Mark, but I realize how uncomfortable and intrusive that would be for you two. So I am once again out."

It was Theo's turn to sigh. He sat down heavily in the chair across from Chris. In the whole scheme of things he realized that Chris was being generous. He could create all sorts of problems for his family if he wanted.

"Couple months ago, my world went haywire. I went through the five stages of grief, I can tell you that. I still struggle with the anger part of it…anger against you, anger against Kelly, and anger against my ministry. I was really angry, but through all of this I was sure of one thing—I was not letting my marriage go. Kelly and I will work this out, what doesn't break us will make us stronger. We were always meant to be together." He ran his hand over his face and glanced at Chris. "You will find your true love one day because she's out there."

Chris snorted. "No disrespect, Theo, but I doubt I will ever love anybody ever again. At least not the way I loved Kelly."

Theo grimaced and then got up. There was an underlying anger toward Chris especially when he spoke about Kelly, and he felt the very real desire to shout, *well good for you, I hope you never find anybody else to love!*

"Whatever you decide, don't forget that God loves you and this whole situation could have been avoided if you had just trusted him and not yielded to temptation."

Chris nodded, a dejected slump to his shoulder. "Thanks, Theo. I know I don't deserve your civility and once again I am truly sorry that you got hurt in this whole thing."

Theo nodded and headed toward the door. "Take care of yourself."

He did not stop to hear Chris' reply. He left the office and walked through the reception area. Slowly he could feel the slow burning anger toward Chris lift. When he got into the car he felt a bit lighter than when he entered.

He drove home slowly, a determined set to his chin. He was going to have a serious talk with Kelly. She needed to understand that this monstrous blow to their marriage could never happen again, must never happen again.

When he entered the house Kelly was lounging on the back patio, reading a book. The children were still at school, so the place was eerily quiet.

He sauntered onto the patio and looked at her. She jumped when she saw him, a half smile playing across her lips. "You startled me. I just put the baby down for a nap and decided to catch up on my reading. Welcome home. It's great to see you." She got up to give him a hug.

He looked at her sternly, a fierce look on his face. "Before you touch me, here are the rules."

Kelly stiffened and sank back down in the chair, a fearful look on her face.

"Number one, you and I will never again let a third party

enter our marriage. Never! You understand me?"

Kelly's eyes watered and she whispered. "I am so sorry about that."

"Number two," he said ignoring her, "you and our three children will be living with me in Cayman. I know you were waiting for me to ask, but I had to be sure I was over the major part of this. I didn't want to have any residual resentment towards you or our youngest child. I can anticipate that in years to come I will feel twinges of betrayal, after all, I am only human, but I cannot just let us go like that. I don't want to start over with someone else. I don't want to be away from you much longer."

She nodded again, wiping away the tears from her eyes though she was smiling, a hopeful look in her eyes.

"Number three," he continued, joining her on the seat, "never ever stop communicating with me, okay? If I get too overbearing, if I stop being the husband you love, tell me... talk to me."

He wiped the tears that were running unchecked down her face with his thumb.

"Yes," she whispered, "I love you Theo, and only you."

"This is no fairytale, Kelly. Happily ever after is for storybooks. I just want to know that we'll hang in there together, you understand me?"

"Yes," Kelly said chokingly.

"I can't hear you," Theo grinned looking at her lovingly. "Are the rules clear and completely understood?"

"Yes," she shouted, getting up and kissing him all over his face. "Yes," she whispered as she kissed him deeply.

THE END

Keep reading for an excerpt from
Loving Mr. Wright, Erica's story

Erica drove into the shrub lined driveway of her sister's former home and felt a surge of loneliness so palpable it hit her like a dull thud somewhere in the region of her heart. Her sister, Kelly, and her family were gone to the Cayman Islands to live and for now, she had volunteered as their house sitter.

It was a job she was happy to do because her apartment, though walking distance from where she worked as a hotel nurse, was really just a glorified studio, and she relished the prospect of living again in a real house with yard space. She glanced over at the lawn. It had just started to sprout some wayward patches of grass and already looked overgrown. A gentle breeze touched the greenery and the clumps of grass seemed to wave at her mockingly—*you cannot take care of a yard as big as this*, they seemed to say to her.

Erica sighed and parked in front of the garage. How would she putter around in a five bedroom, four-bathroom house with almost half an acre of yard space dedicated to flowers and exotic shrubs?

This was a family home. She picked some lint off her jeans. In the past, she was quite happy to visit her sister and lounge on her verandah sipping drinks or scrounging around in her kitchen for food.

Now, here she was, all alone: no children to play with and no sister to argue with. She felt a gaping hole that her sister and her family used to fill and for the first in a long time, she realized that she really had no life.

She worked at the hotel Flamingo as a nurse, where she dispensed painkillers and kept up with the light work. Her job now was a far cry from her duties in the surgical ward. It was now more laid back and less stressful.

That's all she did, work, hang out with her sister's children, occasionally have lunch with her mother, and go to church. She was happily living the life of a spinster, but she had no male prospect on the horizon to get excited about, and nobody to get excited about her.

She looked down at her size 14 jeans balefully. Lately she had been spending way too much time eating. The jeans she had on could barely fit her. She had struggled to get into them this morning and now she was shuddering to think of how she would get out of them.

"Pathetic!" Erica muttered impatiently, taking her box out of the car and heading into the house.

The house felt empty—even though there was furniture in it—as if it knew that the rightful owners were away. She had a plan to cart over a box or two of her belongings every day until she had fully moved in.

She headed toward the guest room at the very end of the hallway upstairs. She was used to staying in that room when she visited in the past and she always thought that it was cooler than the rest of the rooms in the house. It had a balcony, which had an unobstructed view of the town of Ocho Rios. She gazed out of the window for a while and then sat on the bed, staring into space.

Maybe she should call her sister and let her know that she was just starting the moving-in process, but then again, they had left just one week ago and she had spoken to Kelly at least twice per day—asking her questions about Cayman, hanging onto her every word. She really needed to get a life apart from her sister and her family. As the older sister, by four years, she had always thought that she would be the first to get married and have children, but here she was, still single and for the first time in a long time she felt the first stifling stirrings of unhappiness grip her heart; that feeling, that everybody in the world was happier than she was. She thought she had quenched these feelings a long time ago.

She grabbed her cell phone and punched in her mother's

number. The two of them were unusually close for a mother and daughter, maybe because she had nobody else to hang out with. All her friends were married or had children and were too busy raising their families to care about her. Usually she was fine with that, but today she felt slightly down because of her situation.

The phone on her mother's end rang for a while and then a breathless Lola came on the line. "Erica, I thought you would have been down here."

"Where?" Erica frowned slightly. "What are you up to?"

"I'm at church," Lola said, "getting my heart checked, my blood pressure checked and doing an eye test."

"What for?" Erica asked puzzled.

"The medical professionals from church, are doing a free day," Lola said exasperatedly. "Were you not at church when it was announced? Shouldn't you be down here helping? Aren't you a medical professional?"

"Oh, I forgot all about it," Erica said sullenly. "I was just moving in."

"Aah," Lola said soothingly. "You are feeling a bit down."

"Yes," Erica mumbled. "I am missing Kelly and the children a tad bit more than I should. I suddenly feel as if I have no life."

"Do you know what a good remedy for that is?" Lola asked sweetly.

"What mother?" Erica asked suspiciously, "get married, and have my own babies?"

"Nooo…well yes," Lola laughed. "I was thinking that your present situation could be remedied if you come and help out down here. You don't have to go to the hotel until in the evening. Come on down and take your mind off your empty nest."

"Okay," Erica sighed, "might as well."

When she drove into the church parking lot she had her car's AC on full blast and was reluctant to get out of the car. For some reason this summer felt like the hottest on record. However, the full parking lot was an indication that the heat was not a deterrent to people attending the health fair. She could already see, from her vantage point, several white circular tents with signs on the white flaps announcing various medical procedures. The parking lot did not have enough space though and several tents were pitched on the church lawn.

Erica grimaced. Hyacinth Donahue was going to have a fit. Her precious heliconia flower leaves, which she maintained as a matter of pride, and which made for a very colorful hedge, were being used as temporary umbrellas and fans.

There were long lines in front of each tent, and persons were milling around with small packages in hand. She spotted a health food tent and vowed to check it out. Maybe it was time she started eating healthier. The thought made her gag a little, but enough was enough; she hadn't gotten this big because she was eating healthily.

She pushed her hands into her white overcoat; even the short sleeves felt hot.

"Sister Erica, so glad you are here." Dr. Mansoon grinned when he saw her. "You forgot about this, didn't you?"

"Yup," Erica nodded, grinning back at him. "I was talking to my mother on one of my routine calls to her and she reminded me."

"Well," Dr. Mansoon patted his shirt pocket and dragged out a badge with her name on it. "You are not the only one who is missing in action today. I have three more badges. We assigned you to the eye-care booth for routine eye tests—get to working Nurse." He gave her a mock scowl.

"It seems as if the whole town is here," Erica said taking

the badge from him.

He grunted and then spun around when somebody shouted his name. "Got to go."

Erica nodded and made her way to the eye-care booth. It was routine work for her and slightly boring.

Her small booth was supposed to be manned by two nurses but when Sister Darcy saw her coming, she handed the clipboard to Erica and explained the routine. "When the nurse from this booth detects that something is seriously wrong, send them to that booth." She pointed to an adjoining booth. "Write your findings and the doctor over there will take it from there. Simple." She then gave Erica a smirk and said, "Gotta run...have things to do."

After the long line receded from her booth, and mercifully, the sun had receded behind an ominous looking cloud, Erica sat gazing over the parking lot. The community had really taken advantage of the church's initiative to provide free health care. It was something that the medical professionals at the church had wanted to do for a long time.

Erica could barely remember discussing this venture at the last meeting. At the time she was distracted by her sister's unfortunate situation.

She still couldn't believe that Kelly had been brave enough to have had an affair and then had her lover's baby. If she had a husband like Theo she would never, in a million years, have looked at someone else.

She always dreamed of marrying a man like Theo, a man who loves his woman with such a deep abiding love that nothing could shake it.

She exhaled. She was happy that Theo took back Kelly after her extra marital affair, but she still shuddered to think of the long term consequences that the affair would have on the family.

Maybe it was better for her to remain single and unattached than to go through the emotional wringer that relationships seem to offer. She had tried to be the perfect girlfriend to two men in the past, but both times she had to leave the relationship broken hearted.

She had known Corey from high school and he had been her first love but he left her when she became a Christian. "Can't handle the rules," he told her sheepishly. "Christianity is a bag of rules and I am a free thinker."

She moped around for years after that, yearning for a stable Christian man to recognize that she was wife material. Then she met Jay-Jay: Jason Jolly.

He was handsome, had a good job and seemed God-fearing. He had proposed to her on a Tuesday night. She had just gotten off shift from her job at Three Rivers Bay Hospital and he had gone down on one knee.

The Wednesday morning his wife had called her, asking if bigamy was no longer illegal in Jamaica. Erica had been shocked. It had taken her the better part of her thirties, when she still had a semblance of a waist, to get over Jay-Jay.

Now here she was, single and lonely. The kind of loneliness that usually had a single woman of thirty-five—with no real prospects—feeling that she had to do something about her situation.

Obviously, Mr. Right was nowhere near her radius.

OTHER BOOKS BY BRENDA BARRETT

Love Triangle Series

Love Triangle: Three Sides To The Story- George, the husband, Marie, the wife and Karen-the mistress. They all get to tell their side of the story.

Love Triangle: After The End--Torn between two lovers. Colleen married her high school sweetheart, Isaiah, hoping that they would live happily ever after but life intruded and Isaiah disappeared at sea. She found work with the rich and handsome, Enrique Lopez, as a housekeeper and realized that she couldn't keep him at arms length...

Love Triangle: On The Rebound--For Better or Worse, Brandon vowed to stay with Ashley, but when worse got too much he moved out and met Nadine. For the first time in years he felt happy, but then Ashley remembered her wedding vows...

New Song Series

Going Solo (New Song Series-Book 1)- Carson Bell, had a lovely voice, a heart of gold, and was no slouch in the looks department. So why did Alice abandon him and their daughter? What did she want after ten years of silence?

Duet on Fire (New Song Series- Book 2)- Ian and Ruby had problems trying to conceive a child. If that wasn't enough, her ex-lover the current pastor of their church wants her back...

Tangled Chords (New Song Series- Book 3)- Xavier Bell, the poor, ugly duckling has made it rich and his looks have been incredibly improved too. Farrah Knight, hotel heiress had cruelly rejected him in the past but now she needed help. Could Xavier forgive and forget?

Broken Harmony(New Song Series-Book 4)- Aaron Lee, wanted the top job in his family company but he had a moral clause to consider just when Alka, his married ex-girlfriend walks back into his life.

A Past Refrain (New Song Series-Book 5)- Jayce had issues with forgetting Haley Greenwald even though he had a new woman in his life. Will he ever be able to shake his love for Haley?

Perfect Melody (New Song Series- Book 6)- Logan Moore had the perfect wife, Melody but his secretary Sabrina was hell bent on breaking up the family. Sabrina wanted Logan whatever the cost and she had a secret about Melody, that could shatter Melody's image to everyone.

The Bancroft Family Series

Homely Girl (The Bancrofts- Book 0) - April and Taj were opposites in so many ways. He was the cute, athletic boy that everybody wanted to be friends with. She was the overweight, shy, and withdrawn girl. Do April and Taj have a love that can last a lifetime? Or will time and separate paths rip them apart?

Saving Face (The Bancrofts- Book 1) - Mount Faith University drama begins with a dead president and several suspects including the president in waiting Ryan Bancroft.

Tattered Tiara (The Bancrofts- Book 2) - Micah Bancroft is targeted by femme fatale Deidra Durkheim. There are also several rape cases to be solved.

Private Dancer (The Bancrofts- Book 3) Adrian Bancroft was gutted when he returned to Jamaica and found out that his first and only love Cathy Taylor was a stripper and was literally owned by the menacing drug lord, Nanjo Jones.

Goodbye Lonely (The Bancrofts- Book 4) - Kylie Bancroft was shy and had to resort to going to confidence classes. How could she win the love of Gareth Beecher, her faculty adviser, a man with a jealous ex-wife in his past and a current mystery surrounding a hand found in his garden?

Practice Run (The Bancrofts Book 5) - Marcus Bancroft had many reasons to avoid Mount Faith but Deidra Durkheim was not one of them. Unfortunately, on one of his visits he was the victim of a deliberate hit and run.

Sense of Rumor (The Bancrofts- Book 6) - Arnella Bancroft was the wild, passionate Bancroft, the creative loner who didn't mind living dangerously; but when a terrible thing happened to her at her friend Tracy's party, it changed her. She found that courting rumors can be devastating and that only the truth could set her free.

A Younger Man (The Bancrofts- Book 7)- Pastor Vanley Bancroft loved Anita Parkinson despite their fifteen-year age gap, but Anita had a secret, one that she could not reveal to Vanley. To tell him would change his feelings toward her, or force him to give up the ministry that he loved so much.

Just To See Her (The Bancrofts- Book 8)- Jessica Bancroft had the opportunity to meet her fantasy guy Khaled, he was finally coming to Mount Faith but she had feelings for Clay Reid, a guy who had all the qualities she was looking for. Who would she choose and what about the weird fascination Khaled had for Clay?

The Three Rivers Series

Private Sins (Three Rivers Series-Book 1)- Kelly, the first lady at Three Rivers Church was pregnant for the first elder of her church. Could she keep the secret from her husband and pretend that all was well?

Loving Mr. Wright (Three Rivers Series- Book 2)- Erica saw one last opportunity to ditch her single life when Caleb Wright appeared in her town. He was perfect for her, but what was he hiding?

Unholy Matrimony (Three Rivers Series- Book 3) - Phoebe had a problem, she was poor and unhappy. Her solution to marry a rich man was derailed along the way with her feelings for Charles Black, the poor guy next door.

If It Ain't Broke (Three Rivers Series- Book 4)- Chris Donahue wanted a place in his child's life. Pinky Black just wanted his love. She also wanted him to forget his obsession with Kelly and love her. That shouldn't be so hard? Should it?

Contemporary Romance/Drama

The Preacher And The Prostitute - Prostitution and the clergy don't mix. Tell that to ex-prostitute, Maribel, who finds herself in love with the Pastor at her church. Can an ex-prostitute and a pastor have a future together?

New Beginnings - Inner city girl Geneva was offered an opportunity of a lifetime when she found out that her 'real' father was a very wealthy man. Her decision to live up-town meant that she had to leave Froggie, her 'ghetto don,' behind. She also found herself battling with her stepmother and battling her emotions for Justin, a suave up-towner.

Full Circle- After graduating from university, Diana wanted to return to Jamaica to find her siblings. What she didn't foresee was that she would meet Robert Cassidy and that both their pasts would be intertwined, and that disturbing questions would pop up about their parentage, just when they were getting close.

Historical Fiction/Romance

The Empty Hammock- Workaholic, Ana Mendez, fell asleep in a hammock and woke up in the year 1494. It was the time of the Tainos, a time when life seemed simpler, but Ana knew that all of that was about to change.

The Pull Of Freedom- Even in bondage the people, freshly arrived from Africa, considered themselves free. Led by Nanny and Cudjoe the slaves escaped the Simmonds' plantation and went in different directions to forge their destiny in the new country called Jamaica.

Jamaican Comedy (Material contains Jamaican dialect)

Di Taxi Ride And Other Stories- Di Taxi Ride and Other Stories is a collection of twelve witty and fast paced short stories. Each story tells of a unique slice of Jamaican life.

CPSIA information can be obtained at www.ICGtesting.com
Printed in the USA
BVOW04s2349200115

384235BV00015B/123/P